SABOTEUR

Karl Wagner was a fortunate young career diplomat having just been appointed as a military attaché to the German Embassy in Ireland. He could hardly believe his luck. Ireland was a neutral country with an enviable reputation for hospitality, good food and Guinness, and with Britain as a common enemy the Germans were viewed by the majority of the Irish as powerful friends, rather than potential aggressors. He'd heard stories about beautiful Irish colleens and something called 'craic' and by all accounts the pubs in Dublin were the best in the world. His work would be important and if he did it well he'd be assured of promotion but as he settled into his small flat just walking distance from the German Embassy at 58 Northumberland Road, he had to admit to himself that his top priority was to explore the local scene. It was a warm evening when he set off to find the nearest pub which he'd been told was Ryan's Beggars Bush on Haddington Road. He wasn't disappointed. Even at 6pm the atmosphere inside the smoky and noise-filled bar was vibrant with lots of young people sipping pints of Guinness and engaged in deep conversation while at the bar a selection of older regulars stared wistfully into glasses of amber Irish Whiskey. His entrance attracted no attention and only when his accent was detected by the barman did the fact that he was German get noticed.

'*Welcome to Dublin and what can I get you? I'm afraid we don't have any German beers.*' Asked the barman.

'*A pint of Guinness, bitte.*' He said, acknowledging that the barman's insight. '*How did you know I was German? I'm not wearing lederhosen.*'

The barman looked up from the pump and smiled. '*A German with a sense of humour - now there's a thing! What's your name?*'

'*Karl and you're right, I am German and I work at the German embassy. Today is my first day in Dublin.*' he replied.

'*Well Karl, it was a lucky guess.*' He replied. '*But with the German embassy being just around the corner it's odds-on that any foreigner we see in here these days is German.*'

They chatted for a few minutes as the barman poured the pint of Guinness. It was an elaborate procedure where the barman poured a third of the glass from each of three barrels before placing it on the counter.

'Why is it so complicated?' Queried Karl.

'The first third is from a nearly full barrel, the second from a half-full barrel and the last third from a nearly empty barrel. If it was all poured from the first barrel it would be too fizzy and if it was all poured from the nearly empty barrel it would be too flat and it wouldn't have that nice creamy head.' The barman pushed the glass across the bar towards the waiting German and said, *'Your first pint of Guinness?'*

'Yes it is. I've heard a lot about how good it is.' He replied as he lifted the pint glass to his lips but before he could take a sip the barman said, *'Karl, you don't sip Guinness, you to drink at least a quarter of the pint at a time.'*

'We drink our beer in Bavaria that way also.' He responded and with that he proceeded to down half of the glass before placing the glass back on the bar with a satisfied smile. *'That is absolutely delicious.'*

'Be warned,' said the barman *'I understand that Guinness is about twice the strength of a typical German lager. I've seen a few of your colleagues more than a little worse for wear after drinking what they'd thought was well within their capacity.'*

He finished the pint, ordered another and while it was being poured he looked around for a seat at a table where he might be able to join a conversation. Then, as if reading his mind the barman called out to a table close to the bar, *'Hey Mick, Karl here has just downed his first pint of Guinness - he's new at the German embassy - why don't you introduce him to a few of your friends.'*

Soon Karl was engaged in conversation with Mick and his drinking mates. He enjoyed being the centre of attention and when he'd finished his second pint he offered to buy a round for the table. Some sandwiches followed and by the time he'd seen the bottom of his glass for the fourth time he realised he was in danger of getting seriously drunk. The barman was right, the Guinness was going to his head. Meanwhile his new-found friends continued to drink pint after pint without any apparent effect. It was time to go he thought, it wouldn't look good to get falling-down drunk on his first day in Dublin. It was only then that he considered the possibility that one or more of the embassy staff might be witnessing his performance. Suddenly feeling more sober he solemnly thanked everyone for their welcoming company and resisting the instinctive reaction to click his heels and salute he left the pub and walked back to his flat, very thankful for the fresh air.

It was June 1940 and things were going well for the Third Reich. France, Belgium and The Netherlands had all capitulated and been occupied and only Britain stood alone against the might of Germany. The popular view from abroad was that the UK couldn't hold out for long and once the Luftwaffe had gained control of the skies over southeast England Hitler would order the invasion of Britain. At the same time admiral Dönitz's U-boat wolf packs were wreaking havoc on the Atlantic convoys which were bringing vital supplies of food, fuel and armaments from the USA. All things considered, the downfall of Britain looked inevitable and although Ireland was keen to be friends with the probable victor, they had to be careful. Because of its strategic location controlling the Western Approaches to the United Kingdom the Irish Government under Eamon De Valera feared a British invasion. A German invasion was also on the cards but seemed less likely. However in January 1939 and in direct contravention of the Government's carefully crafted neutrality the small but influential Irish Republican Army formally declared war on Britain and days later launched a bombing campaign targeting civil, economic and military infrastructure in England. The Irish Government distanced itself from this action and under British pressure introduced strong measures against the IRA, rushing through the Emergency Powers Act which included internment for IRA suspects and the death penalty for acts of terrorism. At that time the IRA was reduced less than a thousand active members, many of whom were in prison and those who remained were a hard core of the most passionate nationalists who were devoted to the the reunification of Ireland and who would stop at nothing to further their cause. Unsurprisingly they were keen to collaborate with the Germans, even sending an invasion plan for Northern Ireland to German Intelligence. There was no real expectation that this plan would be embraced by the Germans but it did signal the IRA's desire to collaborate and it encouraged the German ambassador in Dublin to establish a secret communications channel with the leadership of the IRA. However it was widely speculated that the Nazis had been supplying arms to the IRA for years although this was always officially denied. In a sense that was 'normal' but if Britain suspected the Irish Government of contravening its neutrality and materially assisting the Germans, then De Valera knew Britain could march across the border from Northern Ireland and occupy the country within days and his struggle for freedom from the British would start all over again. He was at pains to keep the British Government sweet with small concessions like agreeing to repatriate downed RAF pilots to England, while interning their German counterparts. The Germans also chose to tread carefully, officially respecting Ireland's declared neutrality while unofficially continuing to provide low-key support to the IRA in their campaign against the British.

Feeling slightly hungover from his session in the pub the previous night Karl made sure he was at his desk in the German embassy bright and early the following morning. It was the first day in his new job and he wanted to make a good impression. Shortly after 9am he was summoned to the ambassador's office to meet the ambassador and his key members of staff. An orderly opened the door to an office which was decked with the usual Nazi paraphernalia, two flags at the edges of the room flanking the ambassador's oversized desk and two drapes were carefully hung from the ceiling so as to neatly frame him when he was seated at the desk while similarly neatly framing the large portrait photograph of the Fuhrer. It was a photograph he'd seen countless times before, taken with Hitler looking intensely into the camera lens and consequently with the disturbing quality of ensuring that no matter where anyone was in the room Adolf Hitler was looking directly at them. To one side of the office by the window was a group of four chairs arranged in a circle facing a splendid leather wing chair in which sat the German Ambassador to Ireland, Herman Lange. On entering the room the ambassador sprang smartly to his feet and gestured to Karl to join them. He was an impressive silver-haired man probably in his late fifties or early sixties, tall and slim and obviously fit. A thin black moustache matched his black eyebrows and his intense blue eyes suggested a disturbing ability to look straight into one's head. *'Welcome to our team, Karl,'* he said, extending his hand to shake Karl's. It was a firm, dry handshake from a man who was obviously used to commanding attention. *'Thank you Sir.'* Replied Karl with a respectful nod of his head as he took his seat next to the ambassador, relieved at the absence of Heil Hitlers, Nazi salutes and clicking heels. Once the introductions were over there was a brief discussion on the status of the war where the importance of maintaining the best possible relations with Ireland was emphasised. Superficially it was a relaxed meeting but it was clear from the minute he entered the ambassador's office the deference in which he was held. When the meeting ended the ambassador signalled to Karl to remain behind and then as if making a deliberate point, he reseated himself behind his desk indicating to Karl to take the seat directly facing him across the desk. It was clear that the relaxed bonhomie of the previous meeting had left the room with the other members of staff.

After clearing his throat and methodically lighting a cigarette, Herr Lange said, *'I see from your records that you were a star graduate from the Hitler Youth programme and that you have already shone in your early days as an SS officer. You are to be congratulated, however your training and career so far are not very relevant in this job.'* He paused to let the message sink in and then continued, *'I hope you make a success of this posting Karl but I would advise caution on becoming over-friendly with the Irish, particularly in the Beggars Bush. You were watched yesterday evening and while we laud you for the ease with which you made friends it's important to get the balance right. Familiarity is a double-edged sword. I'm sure you will agree that we must never allow the Irish to take advantage of us. We may share a common enemy but you will quickly discover that the Irish are an extremely complicated nation and it would be very simple for an inexperienced operative to step on a political landmine. Karl, you do have a bright future ahead of you but you need to be careful.'* He raised an eyebrow, questioning whether his rebuke had been understood and accepted.

'I understand Sir. It is not an excuse but the Guinness went straight to my head. I apologise and I assure you Herr Ambassador that it will never happen again.' He responded, aware that he'd got off to a less than ideal start to his his new job. However the ambassador's faint smile and slight nod of his head signalled that the issue was over although probably not forgotten.

'I suggest you take a day or two getting to know your colleagues. It's important you understand the Irish as best you can, because you will find out soon enough that our relationship with them is far from straightforward and I'd recommend that the next time you revisit the Beggars Bush you take one of our more experienced members of staff with you - and stick to two pints at most.'

Signalling that the meeting was now over Karl got rose to his feet and feeling Hitler's watchful eyes on him he felt it appropriate to salute before turning smartly and returning to his own office down the hall. Thankfully on his own once again he took stock. The Ambassador had impressed him and although he'd been ticked off for his behaviour he felt that the rebuke had been proportionate. It seemed that his misdemeanour would be overlooked this time but it would be unwise to err again. There seemed to be an integrity about Herr Lange that engendered loyalty and already he was looking forward to serving him to the best of his ability. Karl's thoughts then turned to wondering how he had been observed in the bar the previous night. Was the barman in cahoots with the German embassy? That would certainly make sense from the German perspective but risky for the barman who presumably would have to be well-paid for his services. The barman was perfectly positioned to see everything that was going on in the bar and in Karl's case he knew precisely how much he'd had to drink. But he didn't dismiss the possibility that someone from the embassy had been assigned to watch him and see that he didn't get into trouble. All-in-all he felt happy that he'd done no permanent damage to his prospects as the newly appointed military attaché to the German Embassy so he went off to get himself a cup of coffee and on reentering his office he stopped briefly to admire the brass plate on his door - Karl Wagner, Military Attaché it said.

At the other end of Ireland, about as far from Dublin as one could get, Patrick McGonigle was staring pensively into his pint of Guinness in Roddens Bar in Buncrana wondering what the future held for him. He'd just been made redundant and his prospects of finding another job weren't good. Why he'd been let go was a mystery. The given reason was that they had too many welders for the amount of work they had but he suspected that the new owner had got wind of the fact that he was a member of the IRA. The small engineering company he'd been working for had recently changed hands and the new owner was a hardline Catholic. Patrick was a Protestant and even a minor infringement would have been sufficient reason to fire him but the suspicion of being a member of the IRA would certainly have sealed his fate. It was ironic because although he'd joined the IRA four years ago as a teenager he'd seen no active duty since. Not that he was hungry for action, quite the contrary. In his opinion the IRA's activity in Donegal had done little to advance the nationalist cause and had mainly resulted in the death and injury of innocent bystanders. Despite his belief in a united Ireland he'd recently thought of leaving the organisation but he feared the brutal punishments meted out by the IRA to so-called deserters. Anything from a serious beating to being knee-capped could be expected. The only way out would be to disappear and then emigrate but with the war raging it was nigh-on impossible to get a boat anywhere. It was mid-afternoon and apart from him the bar was empty, as was his glass. He couldn't afford another pint so he said goodbye to the barman and headed out into the sunshine for a walk along the banks of Loch Swilly in the hope that the fresh air might help him decide what to do. He made his way down Swilly Road to the ferry slipway at the northern entrance to the Cranna River and sat down against a low wall to think things over. A gentle southwesterly breeze ruffled the surface of the Lough and the sun glittered and glimmered as he gazed across at the mountains of Donegal to the west. It was warm and the pint of Guinness had made him drowsy so he closed his eyes and before long he had drifted off into a troubled sleep. Some time later he was sharply awakened by someone kicking his foot and a voice saying, *'you better move Patrick, the tide is rising and if you stay here much longer you'll be in the water.'*

It took a few seconds for Patrick to come round before he recognised one of his IRA colleagues that he'd not seen for several weeks. *'Haven't seen you in a while Sean. How did you know I was here? What do you want?'*

'I heard you got sacked,' he replied, *'just thought I check to see how you were doing - any plans?'*

'Not yet. Think I might head down to Dublin. There's no work here.' Said Patrick wearily as they started to stroll back into the town.

'Fancy a pint?' Said Sean.

'Only if you're buying - I'm skint.' He replied.

They strolled slowly back to Roddins Bar and took their drinks to a quiet table in a corner where they were soon joined by several other of his IRA colleagues. They talked in hushed tones for a while about possible targets but the mood was universally negative and as soon as a suggestion was put forward, it would get shot down by someone who invariably opened his salvo with the phrase *'The problem with that is...'* Patrick listened for a while and it slowly dawned on him that there was nothing for him in Donegal, no work and no IRA action. Waiting for a quiet moment he put both hands on the table, stood up and said wearily, *'You guys are all talk. I'm off to Dublin. There's nothing here for me - no work and no action.'* Suddenly feeling better having made a decision on his future he spun round and marched out of the bar already mentally packing for the journey. Two days later he was alighting from the bus at Busáras, the main bus station in Dublin. Collecting his small suitcase from the luggage compartment at the bottom of the bus he walked down to the bridge at Customs House Quay crossed it and headed towards a hostel the bus driver had recommended. He had two immediate objectives, first to find a job and then to get in touch with the IRA. There was a noticeboard in the hostel on which were posted various documents, mostly house rules but also details of upcoming events and one or two job opportunities doing manual work on building sites or serving in local bars and cafés. If he could find some temporary work as soon as possible it would give him time to properly research any opportunities there might be for welders in the numerous engineering companies around the docks. He copied down the details and spent the day walking between locations asking for work. All the time wondering how to make contact with the IRA. He knew that under indirect pressure from the Britain the Irish Government was stamping down hard on the organisation. Many members languished in prison and one or two had been executed for terrorist activity. He kicked himself for not asking the local commander in Donegal to contact his counterpart in Dublin and set up a meeting. By four-thirty that afternoon he was at the junction of Northumberland Road and Haddington Road, foot-weary and still jobless when the rain started. Less than a hundred yards ahead he spotted a hanging sign outside a pub called the Beggars Bush so he made a dash for it and ducked inside. It was almost empty so he sat up at the bar and not being able to afford a full pint of Guinness he self-consciously ordered a half-pint. The look he got from the barman indicated that he suspected as much. *'How's it going mate?'* He said, cheerily. It would have been obvious to even the most casual observer that Patrick was down in the dumps and particularly in Ireland, a barman's role was to cheer people like Patrick up.

'I'm fine, thanks......actually that's not true, I'm not fine. I lost my job a few days ago, I'm broke - hence the half-pint - I've just spent the day hiking around Dublin looking for work without success and it's raining. Apart from all that, I'm fine.' He said, doing what all lonely Irishmen do in a pub, confiding in the barman.

'Tough times. What kind of work are you looking for?' He enquired, pulling himself a half-pint as he spoke.

'I'm a welder but just now I'd take any job on offer. Another two days in the hostel and I'll be completely skint so if I don't find work before then I'll be sleeping rough.' He replied mournfully. *'Sorry, I'm not the best company at the moment but enough of self-pity - how are you doing?'*

'I'm fine,' the barman replied cheerfully, *'Could be busier but what with the war and rationing, people are definitely being more careful with their money. At least Guinness isn't being rationed...yet... The regulars still come in most nights for a drink but they drink less than they used to however they still have to get away from their wives for an hour or two. We have music on Fridays and Saturdays so we're quite busy then.'*

The conversation drifted into politics and the war and after it became obvious that Patrick wasn't going to buy another drink the barman generously poured him half-pint on the house. *'Tell you what,'* he said, *'I could do with a hand behind the bar on music nights if you fancied a bit of table tending and washing glasses? Couldn't pay much but it might tide you over until you find some full-time work.'*

'That would be great!' Said Patrick, *'only if you're sure - I'm not asking for charity.'*

'No no, I've been thinking for a while now that having some help on music nights might pay for itself. When it gets very busy in here our turnover is limited by how fast we can pull pints. Can't pay you much but there'd be tips. Friday, five pm - OK?' He said, stretching across the bar to shake Patrick's hand. *'By the way, my name's Seamus, Seamus O'Malley, I manage the bar.'*

The rain had stopped and the sun was out again as Patrick walked back to the hostel. He had a spring in his step, now he could concentrate on doing the rounds of the engineering companies in the docks where he felt sure there'd be work for a welder. Also, if he did find full time employment he could continue to supplement his income by working at the Beggars Bush on music nights. Bright and early the next morning Patrick set off to look for work and aware of the importance of first impressions he'd tidied himself up as best he could. The Hostel owner had given him a list of the engineering companies around the docks and his plan was to spend the day knocking on doors. There was an agency in the city which helped the out-of-work find a job but that was for later. Since the previous day's success at the Beggars Bush he was feeling lucky.

The German Embassy was a hive of activity. Even in wartime the round of lavish receptions in the various embassies continued unabated and the following week it was the turn of the Germans. All the foreign ambassadors and their deputies were invited, along with Irish luminaries and socialites from the Government, the services, the private sector and the arts. In the run-up to the reception the Ambassador held a daily meeting at 9am where every detail was meticulously honed to perfection and then tracked to ensure that on the day, nothing went wrong. At first it seemed to Karl that it was all a huge waste of money but he quickly realised that this was how the embassy worked. It was made absolutely clear to all the embassy staff that this reception was not a social event. It was business. First and foremost it was the public face of the German Nation and the image that was to be projected was of the utmost importance, consistent to the last detail with the values and policies of the Third Reich. Second was the importance of networking where every snippet of information or gossip would be logged and analysed for its potential use at some later date. Each member of staff had a designated list of connections they had to get round during the evening. Nobody was to waste time talking to their friends and any conversation was to be politely terminated when it was felt there was no information of any value forthcoming. It was a military campaign, planned with impressive precision. Karl's role as the Military Attaché was to seek out his counterparts in the other embassies and glean whatever information he could about their operations in Ireland, both official and covert. Of course it was the latter that was of most interest but that information would almost never be volunteered without a quid pro quo. That was the tricky bit and being new to the game the advice Karl received from the Ambassador couldn't have been clearer - use this occasion purely to get to know the other attachés personally and more important, make as many contacts with the Irish government officials as possible. It went without saying that a prime target was the British where beneath the veneer of diplomatic civility the two nations were at war. When conversing with the Irish Government officials the embassy staff were strongly advised that any dialogue about the Irish Republican Army was strictly taboo. Finally, there would be sanctions for anyone who visibly drank too much however, encouraging a guest to over-imbibe was encouraged as the alcohol would loosen their tongues. The Ambassador pointed out that it was best to assume that all the other embassies and guests were going through the same process in preparation for the reception. It was all a big game but one where the stakes couldn't have been higher. Following the reception the Ambassador had to prepare a summary report to be wired directly to the desk of Joachim von Ribbentrop, Foreign Secretary of the Third Reich and one of Hitler's closest advisors. Each attendee from the embassy had to have his or her report on the Ambassador's desk by noon on the day following the reception and the final report to Ribbentrop would be wired by five pm the same day. Karl began to consider staying off alcohol altogether but instinctively he knew that would put anyone he was trying to pump for information on their guard. He thought about proposing to the Ambassador that they made some alcohol-free champagne available but held back. It would have almost certainly been suggested before and also he rather liked champagne, especially when he didn't have to pay for it.

When the morning status meeting was closed the Ambassador nodded to Karl and asked him to remain behind for a few minutes. *'Karl, this will all be very new to you and as this is your first formal embassy reception please stay close to me so I can introduce you to people I think you ought to meet and it will also allow me to involve you in discussions which you might need to follow up. I hardly need to tell you to be extra careful when you are talking to anyone from the British Embassy and under no circumstances participate in any talk about the IRA with anyone. The British are paranoid about them and are exerting maximum pressure on the Dáil Éireann to bear down on the IRA who of course are their sworn enemies - as are we, so it's not hard to see where the paranoia comes from. Finally, as my military attaché you will wear your SS uniform but without your cap. Your counterparts from the other embassies will be then able to recognise you immediately and most if not all of them will approach you and introduce themselves - make sure you look your best.'*

'I understand Herr Ambassador.' Karl replied with a tingle of excitement. He was looking forward to the game. That evening in his apartment he spent a long time pressing his uniform and polishing his buttons and boots. He was determined to impress.

The first guests started to arrive at the German Embassy around 6pm and before long the main reception area was buzzing. Each guest was formally announced by a member of the embassy staff and then introduced to the ambassador and his wife, this was despite the fact that almost everyone knew everyone else following the continuous round of monthly diplomatic receptions. The ambassador made a short welcoming speech while Karl took up his predetermined position by the drinks table where he rather self-consciously sipped his champagne. He was being extra careful not to drink too fast, something he wasn't finding easy while standing there on his own. It wasn't long before he was joined by the Italian military attaché, a suave, aristocratic and immaculately dressed signore, dripping with gold braid and and several rows of medals. Italy had only just entered the war on the side of the Germans and like many of his countrymen Karl held the cynical opinion that Mussolini waited until France fell and it looked certain that Germany would soon be masters of all Europe before he threw his hat in the ring. The SS uniform was smart but dowdy compared to his Italian counterpart's. Karl thought it would be good if the Italians could fight as well as they dressed.

Karl clicked his heels and introduced himself, *'My name is Karl Wagner.'*

'I am Guiseppe Riverso,' said the Italian with a slightly louder click of his heels and a smile, *'Nice to meet you Karl, are you a music lover by any chance?'*

Remembering his ambassador's advice he resisted the temptation to enquire about the Italian's preferred direction of travel on the battlefield, instead replying, *'As a matter of fact yes I do love music but my preference is Puccini - my favourite opera is Madame Butterfly. One day I dream of seeing it performed at La Scala.'*

They made small talk for a few minutes before the conversation inevitably turned to the war, *'How long do you think it will be before Britain crumbles?'* Questioned his be-medalled companion in a voice loud enough to have been overheard by the British military attaché who he'd notice was engaged in conversation with a small group of Americans. Karl smiled broadly and diplomatically replied, *'It would be a brave man to make any predictions on that. The new Prime Minister Winston Churchill doesn't appear to be a man who is likely to crumble. Now if you will excuse me, my Ambassador has just signalled that he wants to talk to me. It's been a pleasure to meet you Guiseppe, I'm sure we'll be meeting again before too long.'* It was a bare-faced lie but he needed to politely ease his way out of this conversation and there were many more guests that he had to meet. He nodded courteously to the Italian and walked over to the Ambassador who was heading across the room towards the Anglo-American group while the Italian refilled his glass.

'Come with me Karl, I'll introduce you to the enemy!' He said with a wry smile on his face, *'I see you've already met our Italian ally.'*

By the time the final guest left the embassy later that evening Karl was worn out. Apart from trying to remember the names of his counterparts from the other embassies and consulates, he was struck by how hard it had been to hold a meaningful conversation with anybody while keeping within the guidelines he'd been given by the ambassador in his pre-reception briefing. There were political landmines and trapdoors everywhere. Even the most innocent question could conceal a hidden agenda so already he was learning how to gently steer a conversation towards safety without it being too obvious. This was not to say that meaningful communications were not taking place at the reception. It was universally accepted that every embassy had spies on the payroll, indeed it was widely assumed that his job as a military attaché was simply a cover for espionage and the diplomatic reception played a very important role in the spying game. It was the perfect communications hub for exchanging secret information under the blanket protection of diplomatic immunity and it was also regularly used to identify potential double agents. Herr Lange, the ambassador, was a smooth operator spending most of his time with the senior Irish politicians trying to glean as much information about their dealings with the British as possible. Karl had observed that the British delegation were especially careful to mark the German ambassador when he was talking to the Tánaiste, the deputy head of the Irish Government. Judging by their easy and relaxed interaction Karl deduced that they were friends. The Irish Prime Minister, the Taoiseach and the President of Ireland were always on the invitation list but it was unusual for either to attend.

Afterwards, the ambassador thanked the members of staff warmly for making the reception a success and he then reminded each of the department heads that their report was to be on his desk by noon the next day. It was 1am by the time Karl got back to his flat and despite being very tired, after carefully hanging up his uniform he sat down at his desk and spent the next hour preparing his report. Only then did he collapse into his bed and instantly fall fast asleep.

At more or less the same time Patrick McGonigle had also just collapsed into his bed at the hostel. He'd had an exhausting day knocking on the doors of dockland engineering companies and garages asking for a job. His final visit was to the British and Irish Steam Packet Company which among other services ran the Dublin to Liverpool ferry and to his absolute delight he'd been offered a job. Back in February one of their ferries, the Munster, had hit a German mine close to Liverpool during the night and sunk. Amazingly all two hundred and fifty passengers were saved but Ireland was a net exporter and by far the country's biggest trading partner was Britain, so the loss of the Munster was immediately felt and the company was put under pressure to expedite her replacement. The export revenue was vital to Ireland and the Irish food were no less vital to Britain. This put Ireland in a very tricky position viz-a-viz their declared neutrality and although Germany generally respected this political position there was an ever-present danger of being torpedoed, despite being emblazoned with massive tricolours painted on all Irish steamship topsides. Patrick was offered a three-month trial as a welder on the maintenance crew working shifts and if his work was up to standard during that probationary period the foreman assured him he would get a full time job. When Patrick fell asleep that night he wasn't just content with finding work on his very first day, he was also drunk. On leaving the Irish Steam Packet Company he'd headed directly to the Beggars Bush to tell Seamus O'Malley his only friend in Dublin the good news and to reassure him that despite having secured a full-time job he wanted to continue helping out in the bar on music nights. The Guinness flowed freely and it was a happy man that staggered out into the rain at closing time that evening. He got soaked but he barely noticed it.

The three months probation period flew by and during that time Patrick earned an enviable reputation as a first class welder who could operate in the most difficult, cramped and even dangerous places. With his steady income he moved out of the hostel and found himself a small one-bedroom flat walking distance from his work. He still helped out at the Beggars Bush on Friday and Saturday nights, more because the craic was good than because he needed the money. Despite the war and the rationing, the bar still buzzed at the weekends and all the time his circle of friends grew.

Meanwhile in Britain the German threat had receded as winter approached and conditions for a seaborne invasion became impossible. The RAF had successfully weathered the Luftwaffe attack on the airfields in what Churchill had labelled the Battle of Britain but now Goering's efforts were directed at the major cities and in particular London which was blitzed with devastating results on fifty-seven consecutive days and nights. At sea the Atlantic convoys from America were suffering increasing losses and all the time Ireland walked the tightrope of neutrality, constantly trying to appear even-handed to both sides but not always succeeding. The Irish Government knew that the IRA was secretly working with elements inside Germany to secure their arms and explosives and they were aware that Germany was unofficially supported the IRA both in principle and in material shipments of arms and explosives. It was common knowledge that for a lengthy period during the summer of 1940 Sean Russell, the IRA's Chief of Staff had been in Germany where he was given diplomatic immunity and entertained as a high-ranking diplomat. Unfortunately for the IRA his visit came to naught when he died on the German submarine U-65 a hundred miles from Galway and was buried at sea. Rumour had it that he'd met Ribbentrop with a view to securing an arms supply with which to continue the bombing campaign in Britain.

During those dark months of the war it seemed obvious to most Irishmen that a German victory was inevitable as long as the United States didn't join in the fight against the Nazis. The IRA's sworn objective was to reunite Ireland and there was little doubt that this was high on the agenda for Russell's alleged meeting with Ribbentrop. Although the USA was maintaining its policy of isolationism it was plain that President Roosevelt's sympathies lay with Britain, however other tides swirled in his government and more broadly across the USA where the IRA had many sympathisers, both passive and active. IRA fund-raising campaigns in the US were always successful amongst the large Irish immigrant population but converting those funds into arms was much more difficult and it was for this reason that the IRA turned their attention towards the Nazis with whom they shared nothing other than a common enemy. The Irish Government had little option but to continue to stamp down hard on the IRA and since the enactment of the Emergency Powers many members had been interned and a few were facing execution.

Patrick had all but forgotten about his IRA membership since moving away from Donegal. Although he still believed passionately in the IRA's goal of a united Ireland the risk of internment deterred him from trying to contact the organisation. He also deliberately chose not to get involved in any discussion on the subject and this required considerable skill as there was always a whiff of the IRA in the Beggars Bush. In Patrick's opinion the bombing campaign in Britain seemed of little consequence and usually only resulted in the death of a few innocent civilians. To him it was distasteful and counterproductive to kill bystanders and although it might have kept the IRA torch alight the bombings were little more than an irritant to the British. It was inconceivable to him that the IRA campaign would do anything more than strengthen the British resolve to keep Northern Ireland in the United Kingdom.

In the German embassy Karl was becoming bored. After the reception things quietened down and apart from a briefing by the ambassador on the meeting between Ribbentrop and the Sean Russell, the IRA's Chief of Staff, little of any consequence had happened. The Germans seemed to be winning the war on every front although they'd missed the opportunity to invade England that year. London was being pulverised by the Luftwaffe and the talk was that British morale was low and Churchill might lose his popular support for continuing the war. In the north Atlantic between June and October 1940 the German U-boats ran amok sinking two hundred and seventy ships. Dönitz's U-boat captains and their crews became popular heroes throughout Germany and it was a widely held view that thanks to their heroics in the Atlantic Britain would soon be starved into submission.

Then out of the blue a wire came through from the office of Joachim von Ribbentrop which changed everything. Karl was summoned urgently to the Ambassador's office. *'Come in, Karl and please sit down. We have something important to discuss.'* He said as he moved from behind his desk to sit in his favourite wing-chair by the window, indicating to Karl to sit opposite him. *'Coffee and biscuits are on the way.'* It was obvious this wasn't going to be a short meeting.

'What we are about to discuss is top secret and with the embassy only you and I will know about it. Do you understand?' He said gravely.

'Yes Herr ambassador.' Karl replied, tingling with excitement at the prospect of becoming involved in something big and flattered that the

ambassador had chosen him to confide in. The refreshments arrived and were place on the table between them. When the orderly had left the room and they were alone the ambassador settled himself and continued. *'We have been given the opportunity to deal a heavy blow to Britain. As you know our U-boats are operating successfully in the north Atlantic and in the past four months they have sunk over two hundred and fifty ships carrying food and armaments from the United States of America to Britain. While the Luftwaffe continues to bomb the major cities in England into submission our strategy is to also starve the country by stepping up our assault on the convoys but as time goes on the Royal Navy's escorting vessels, frigates and corvettes are becoming more successful at hunting down our submarines and it is here that Admiral Dönitz has asked for our help.'* He paused to take a sip of his coffee before continuing, *'We have received intelligence that the large shipyard in Belfast called Harland and Wolff has set up a production line to build Royal Navy corvettes to serve as escorts for the north Atlantic convoys. A corvette is smaller than a frigate which in turn is smaller than a destroyer, but it is fast and has the capability to attack a U-boat with depth charges. Harland and Wolff launched the first of these new corvettes at the end of October, just a few days ago and from now on a new corvette will be launched every three or four days. Admiral Dönitz, the senior submarine officer in the Kriegsmarine who is in charge of all U-boat operations in the north Atlantic, has requested that we come up with a plan to sabotage this production line.'*

'Surely the Luftwaffe could bomb the shipyard Herr ambassador?' said Karl as the ambassador took another sip of his coffee.

'The focus of attention of the Luftwaffe is currently on London which is having hundreds of tons of bombs dropped on it every night. The Fuhrer is convinced that the spirit of the British will be broken when London is razed to the ground, so this mission to disable the corvette production line cannot be accomplished with a bombing raid on the shipyard. We have to find another way to put this production line out of action.' Said the ambassador as he carefully nibbled another pfeffernüsse biscuit. *'These are my favourite biscuits and what you see here on the plate is the last of them we'll see for a while.'* He said ruefully. *'Rationing, Karl, after these have been finished we will have to*

start experimenting with Irish biscuits. I understand that Garibaldis are quite popular among the Irish - maybe it would be appropriate to give them a try, don't you think?'

'Yes sir, of course!' responded Karl, pleased that his boss had cracked a joke with him.

The ambassador finished his biscuit and offered the last one on the plate to Karl who dutifully refused it. 'Thank you Karl, I appreciate your generosity but I insist you have it.'

'Much appreciated sir,' he said as he politely took the biscuit. 'I wish I could help but in truth I have no idea how we could sabotage the Harland and Wolff production line.'

'There is an angle that we have been authorised to explore, one where you can play an important role.' Said the ambassador leaning forward as though to avoid being overheard. 'The IRA might be able to help us and I've been authorised to offer them arms and munitions in exchange for their support. But we will have to be very careful that any dealings we have with the IRA remain unseen by the Irish Government who are determined to eradicate them. Not that they ever will, the harder they crack down on the IRA the more determined they seem to become.' He paused again and looked meaningfully at Karl who was beginning to realise the role he would have to play in this scheme. 'Karl, I want you to contact the IRA here in Dublin and set up a meeting where we can discuss possibilities. We have no direct links to the IRA so you will have to make the connection on your own. In any case, it's best this way because if the Irish Government gets to hear that someone from the embassy is working with the IRA, I can deny all knowledge of it and your assignment here will be immediately terminated. What I'm saying Karl, is that on this project you are working directly for German Military Intelligence, the Abwehr and not the embassy. In this way we will minimise any risk to our diplomatic relationship with the Irish Government. Is that clear?'

'Yes sir - perfectly clear. Despite remaining at arm's length, I presume you will still want to be kept up to speed?' Said Karl.

'Most certainly and I may also be able to give you some advice from time to time.' Replied the ambassador, smiling broadly. 'This is a real opportunity for you Karl but it is dangerous. Your work could make a big *different to the war effort but remember nobody in the embassy is to know of this - ok?'*

Karl nodded politely, it was an order not a question. The ambassador stood up and the meeting was over. Karl saluted and returned to his office where he shut the door and sat down to digest the task he'd just been given. He had no idea where to start. That night he was unable to sleep, tossing and turning for hours until finally he fell deeply asleep shortly before the dawn only to be rudely awakened by the alarm a few minutes later. He dressed and after grabbing a cup of espresso coffee in the embassy kitchen he went out for a walk to clear his head and also to avoid having to talk to any of his colleagues. Not only was he on his own but he'd also have to behave in a way which didn't arouse suspicion.

It was a cold and clear morning and the fresh air felt good as he headed towards the river. For a while he thought only about how to keep all this to himself, leaving the bigger problem of how to establish contact with the IRA leadership until later. It soon became clear that he could only do this if he wasn't based at the embassy where he knew it would be next to impossible not to arouse the curiosity of the embassy staff so by the time he reached the river he'd made his mind up, he would take his vacation and stay clear of the embassy for two weeks. That decision taken he turned his attention to the problem of how to make contact with the IRA in a way which would not invite the attention of the Irish authorities. As he walked along the river bank watching the early morning sun gleaming brightly on the Liffey, a plan gradually formed in his head. Being on vacation would give him the excuse to visit many of the city's tourist attractions, taking him to lots of public places where if he kept his eyes and ears open there was a chance he could pick up a lead. It felt like a very thin plan but in the absence of anything else it would have to do. Back at the embassy the ambassador complimenting Karl on it. *'This is a difficult assignment Karl but I'm confident you can handle it but take care, the IRA have a brutal reputation and you will need your wits about you. Remember, I'm here if you need me. In the meantime I will tell the Abwehr you are going underground and not to expect anything from you for up to two weeks.'*

For the rest of that day and into the night Karl mapped out a circuit of the most popular tourist destinations in Dublin. His plan was to concentrate his efforts at the busiest times of the day and then in the evenings systematically visit the bars in the centre of town in the hope of contacting the IRA. After three futile but enjoyable days he was beginning to realise that his 'thin' plan wasn't going to work and as he walked between city's the art galleries and museums and then went to pub after pub he concluded that sooner or later he'd have take the risk of putting it about that he wanted to meet the IRA. Still without any success he decided to take the plunge and where better than in his local, the Beggars Bush. Since he'd arrived in Dublin he'd got to know the barman who seemed to be on first name terms with almost everyone in the pub. It was Friday night and the bar was busy with a traditional Irish folk band playing in the corner, Karl squeezed his way to the bar and ordered a drink, *'Good evening Seamus, I would like a pint of Guinness please - and if you had a quiet moment I'd like a private word with you?'*

'Sure,' the barman replied, *'but it might be a while. As you can see the place is jumping and my helper, Patrick hasn't arrived yet. When he gets here I might be able to take a short break. I'll let you know - in the meantime enjoy your pint.'*

Shortly afterwards Patrick arrived and when Karl had finished his pint, Seamus gave him a nod to follow him down to the taproom. *'Patrick, you mind the fort while I change the barrel of pump number 3, it's running low.'* They descended a flight of stairs to the taproom where Seamus busied himself swapping over the empty barrel for a full one. As he worked he said, *'OK Karl, how can I help you?'*

Unable to think of a way of easing into the question, Karl chose to jump right in, *'Seamus, I would like to talk to someone in the IRA. Do you know any of them?'*

Seamus froze, *'Pardon? Did I hear you correctly? You think I might know someone in the IRA?'* He said, obviously shaken by the question.

'Yes, Seamus, I was hoping you might have a contact name?' Responded Karl, now fully aware that he was in too deep to back out. *'I've no wish to compromise you so if you do give me a lead I swear I won't say it came from you.'*

Seamus had now recovered from the shock and he replied calmly, *'I know nobody in the IRA and I'd advise you to be very careful making enquiries like this. The IRA is a banned organisation, hunted fiercely on both sides of the border. To be a member means internment and even to know a member without passing their name to the authorities also risks imprisonment.'* He tightened up the nut on the pipe which led to the pump above them in the bar and hurried back upstairs with Karl close behind.

'What was that all about?' Queried Patrick as the pair emerged from the taproom.

'Only a crazy German wanting to see what an Irish taproom looked like.' Lied Seamus, unable to think of anything more credible to say.

Embarrassed by the exchange, Karl said goodbye and headed out into the night. Taking stock he concluded it had been a very clumsy exchange on his part and even if Seamus did know some members of the IRA it was highly unrealistic to expect him to hand over their contact details to a German military attaché. The following day, with no alternative plan Karl repeated the fruitless rounds of public galleries and museums but in the evening he decided not to return to the Beggars Bush, instead he strolled down to Lower Bridge Street and the oldest pub in Dublin, the Brazen Head, which he noted from the plaque above the door had existed on this site since 1198. It seemed incredible to him that people had been drinking in this pub since the time of the Papal Bull which launched the era of the Inquisition.

Inside, the atmosphere was thick with smoke and noise and very similar to every other pub in Dublin. Feeling depressed at his failure to make any contact with the IRA and wondering how he would face the barman in the Beggars Bush again he made his way through the throng to the bar and ordered his usual pint of Guinness. He smiled when he thought that at least his plan was giving him plenty of opportunities to enjoy his favourite drink. Looking around him it was easy to imagine the pub was a hotbed of IRA sympathisers. Groups of men were huddled around tables immersed deeply in conversation, drinking pints and smoking and setting the world to rights as only the Irish can. He was envious, a German was only marginally more acceptable to the average Irishman than a Brit, he was also feeling depressed at his singular lack of progress. A week into his first big job as military attaché to the German Embassy and on his current trajectory he was heading for a dismal failure. It was time for him to seek help from the ambassador, a transparent admission of failure but better to do it now than wait for another week to pass without progress. The decision taken he finished his pint, thanked the barman and left the pub for the half-hour walk back to his flat. He was about halfway home when he became aware that a slow moving car appeared to be tracking him. As he glanced back he saw the car begin to gradually accelerate so assuming all was well he turned and unconcerned he continued his walk home. But he never got there. As the car drew level with him it screeched to a halt, two men leapt out and bundled him unceremoniously into the back seat of the car. He was powerless to resist and squashed between his two assailants the car sped off into the night. Not a word was spoken during the long drive out of the city and up into the Wicklow Hills. Eventually the car pulled off the main road onto a hedge-lined dirt track and ten minutes later they arrived at an unlit cottage. The driver unlocked the front door and switched on the lights as Karl was escorted inside to a bare room furnished with only a wooden table and four chairs. He had no sooner taken a seat before the questions started.

'Well Fritz, word is that you wanted to make contact with the IRA. I can't say you were very subtle in your approach but here we are anyway. So let's hear what you want?' Said one of the men who Karl had already suspected from his behaviour was the leader.

'Yes,' replied Karl, 'I do want to meet the IRA. I am the military attaché at the German Embassy and I have the authority of the German Abwehr - that's the German Military Intelligence - to make a proposal to you. Obviously we need to be certain of the utmost secrecy…'

'A statement of the bleeding obvious Fritz. What's the proposal?'

In the next half hour Karl described the situation with the corvette production line in the Harland and Wolff shipyard in Belfast and how important it was to the German war effort to sabotage the line.

'That's a big job, Fritz.' Said the lead IRA man.

'Actually my name isn't Fritz, it's Karl.' Interrupted the German.

'Oh, is it now? You're all Fritz to us,' he said with a snigger and a glance across at his colleagues. *'That's a big job you know - very big. If we do take it on there'll need to be a lot in it for us. What's the offer?'*

'Plenty,' said Karl *'but before we talk numbers I need to have a viable plan to show my superiors but I've been assured that if it is acceptable we will supply you the armaments which your ex-leader Sean Russell had arranged before his untimely death on a German U-boat in August last year.'*

'How do we know you're not working for the British or the Irish?' Questioned the leader who was the only member of the team that had spoken so far. Suddenly alert to the danger it hit him like a blow to the head that he should have anticipated this question and prepared himself for it. Now he was caught naked in the headlights and lost for an answer. *'I don't know.'* He replied, dumbly. *'I can't prove I'm not a British or an Irish agent.'*

There was a long silence before the leader spoke again and this time his voice was full of menace, *'There are several ways we could handle this question Fritz. We could trust you and see where it takes us, we could assume right now that you are a spy and shoot you or we could put you under a little bit of pressure to see if you are telling the truth. Do you know what a knee-capping is, Fritz?'* He said, leaning across the table and looking intensely into Karl's eyes. Karl's mind raced. Already he could see that it looked extremely unlikely they would accept his word at face value so he was either going to be tortured or killed outright. Suddenly short of breath he gulped and replied, choosing his words with the utmost care, *'It is clear that if there is ever going to be collaboration between us we will have to trust each other at some stage. I understand why you might think I am a double-agent and as I've said, I can't prove I'm not but both the IRA and Germany have a lot to gain by working together against the common enemy.'* He paused, took a deep breath and then continued, *'The Third Reich has already shown it wants to work with the IRA but that deal never happened because of the untimely sickness and death of your Chief of Staff. We still want to work with you and this is the perfect campaign where both sides get what they want - you, the arms and explosives you need to continue the struggle for a united Ireland and we get the chance to impact the production of escort vessels for the north Atlantic convoys. Already both sides have taken risks just to get to this point and if you kill me now the embassy will know it was the IRA who did it. Then you will make an enemy of Germany and the Abwehr and you will not get your arms. Germany is winning the war and I'd expect the IRA would want to be on the winning side when Britain falls. The ball is in your court.'*

At this the leader nodded slightly to one of his colleagues who produced a length of rope and proceeded to tie Karl securely to the chair. Then without saying a word the three of them left the room leaving Karl alone. He knew that the IRA could kill him without a second thought if they suspected he was an agent of either the British or the Irish. They might also torture him to see if his story held up under pressure. Briefly he marvelled at his naivety and he kicked himself for being entirely unprepared for the situation he found himself in when it seemed that he could have predicted it from the outset. However he felt that with his last little speech he'd given a good account of himself so all he could do now was to wait and see what the three IRA men decided.

As this was happening, back at the embassy a nervous aide was trying to explain how the last he'd seen of the man he'd been tailing for a week was seeing him being bundled into a car and driven off into the night. The ambassador marked his card sternly before saying, *'Now all we can do is wait and see if the IRA contact us to try to verify Karl's story. I'd say there is a possibility he is already dead. These days the IRA can't afford to take chances. You are dismissed.'* The aide clicked his heels, saluted smartly and left the room suspecting that his dressing down by the ambassador would not be the last he would hear of it, while the ambassador was left pondering the question of what if anything he could do. One thing he realised straightaway was that it would be some time before he saw Karl again. The IRA were bound to hold onto him until a plan was agreed and if a plan was not agreed then the prospects of him being released in one piece were indeed slim. At the very least he would have to inform the Abwehr about Karl's abduction but what slant should he put on his briefing? He could say this was to be expected and he was confident that the situation would be resolved when the IRA understood what they had to gain from collaborating on the plan to sabotage Harland and Wolff. But if it all fell through he'd have failed and he would be accused of negligence for not keeping track of Karl's movements. After two cups of coffee and an hour alone in his office chewing the issue over in his mind he decided to do nothing. It would take a day or two before the IRA decided what to do and then, assuming they wanted to explore the proposal, they would have to contact him. He would wait and see what happened before reporting back to the Abwehr that Karl had been taken. In the meantime he knew that Karl was in a perilous situation and there was absolutely nothing that he could do about it.

In the cottage in the Wicklow Mountains a heated debate was taking place between the three IRA men. Their leader, Liam O'Donnell was adamant that the opportunity was too good to pass up, whereas both his colleagues were deeply concerned. *'Liam, I think this is far too risky for us at the moment. With all the pressure we're under from the Irish, anything other than a quick in-out bombing campaign on the UK mainland is far too dangerous.'* Said Declan Murphy, his vastly experienced henchman. *'Blowing up a border post or a protestant pub is simple compared to trying to disable a shipyard. To do that we'd need to have at least one experienced operative working in Harland and Wolff - someone who knew where to plant the explosives to cause the maximum amount of damage. How would we do that? Granted it would be fantastic to pull it off but...'* before he could finish Liam interrupted him, *'Jazus Declan, why are you always so negative? If you applied your brain to thinking of ways to make this work rather than listing all the problems with it, we might actually get somewhere. This could be a fantastic opportunity, not only to rearm the IRA but also to really hurt the British for a change when all our recent campaigns have done little more than annoy them. What do you think Connor?'* He said, turning to his other colleague.

'Fritz is obviously wet behind the ears but I think he's genuine. The idea of striking a blow against the British in one of their major shipyards is very exciting and the fact that shipyard is in the North makes it irresistible to me. However as Declan has said, it would be a very risky undertaking but with a huge payback if we could pull it off.' Said Connor

with raised eyebrows, *'Morale among our colleagues isn't high at the moment but this could really lift it - don't you think?'*

Feeling slightly bruised by Liam's criticism, Declan chipped in, *'I agree with Connor that the German is probably genuine - it would be a bit strange if he was working for Military Intelligence. We should at least take it to the high command, don't you think? - and let them make the decision.'*

Suddenly decisive, Liam put his hands on the table and stood up, *'Right. That's what we'll do. Declan, you will stay and guard the German while Connor and I go back into Dublin and advise the Chief of Staff that we think the offer to collaborate is genuine. I don't know how long we'll be but make sure you keep your eye on the German - if he's genuine then he'll not want to escape until he's heard if we're going to collaborate or not. But keep him tied to the bed just to be sure.'*

The hour's drive back into Dublin was done mostly in silence, Liam had a lot to think about. His colleagues didn't know it but there were the beginnings of suspicions that the Chief of Staff wasn't wholly trustworthy. Dark rumours were circulating that he was an informant of the Irish Garda Síochána. It was either that or unusually bad luck that followed Stephen Hayes around. Although he had masterminded a plan, codenamed 'Kathleen', which proposed a German invasion of Northern Ireland supported by the IRA, this plan had mysteriously been discovered by the Irish. Not surprisingly this had raised suspicion about Hayes' loyalty to the cause but there was no evidence to directly implicate him and so for the time being his position was secure. However Liam's mind was in turmoil about the possibility that revealing what appeared to be a great opportunity for the IRA to the Chief of Staff might not be such a good idea. There were others in the high command who he knew personally, in particular Pearse Kelly the commanding officer of the Belfast Battalion and as he neared Dublin he thought that it would make sense to talk to him first. He could easily defend this decision by highlighting that if the plan went ahead it would be the Northern Irish branch of the IRA that would be most involved. He'd rather it was up to Kelly to decide whether or not to take it to the Chief of Staff. The decision made he chose to keep it to himself, not that he didn't trust Connor but the fewer people who knew about this the better. He'd rather that word didn't reach Stephen Hayes that he'd chosen to approach Kelly first. Although he had a rationale for his decision it would raise suspicions about his loyalty to the Chief of Staff. Liam was one of the longest serving members of the IRA and he could see how the intense pressure from the Irish Government was systematically eroding the trust in the organisation. In spite of the brutal punishment meted out to informers it was beyond doubt that they were still active within the IRA. Pearse Kelly had inducted him into the IRA almost twenty years ago and since then they had worked on several campaigns together. This opportunity to collaborate with the Germans had so much potential he couldn't risk it being compromised at birth. The IRA was on the ropes and this high profile operation, were it to succeed, would surely fuel a resurgence in the movement? The next question on Liam's mind was whether to discuss it with Kelly over the phone or travel to Belfast to meet him in person. Either way he'd have to give him a call but already he felt a sense of ownership of the project and if he was to have any serious involvement in it, he figured it would be better to meet Kelly in person. it was late by the time they reached Dublin so after the lengthy silence Liam said, *'Connor, I'm going to drop you at your house. Usual time at the Beggars Bush tomorrow evening?'*

'Righto Liam, see you tomorrow. This could be a big operation - just what we need just now.' Said Connor.

Shortly afterwards Liam stopped outside Connor's house, *'Good job Connor. Thanks. See you tomorrow.'* He said as watched his colleague unlock his front door and go inside. He drove the remaining mile to his own home where he phoned Pearse Kelly who answered almost immediately. Liam introduced himself, *'Pearse, Liam here. You probably heard that we'd abducted the military attaché at the German Embassy in Dublin. He's been trying to contact the IRA to discuss an ambitious plan for us to sabotage the Harland & Wolff shipyard in exchange for an unspecified quantity of arms and munitions. I thought I'd better call you first.'*

'Liam, good to hear from you and thanks for the call, if you're sure he's not working with the Garda and his offer to collaborate is genuine then we need to discuss it face-to-face. Can you come up to Belfast in

the next couple of days?' Queried the Battalion Commander, 'and bring the German with you.'

'I'll see you in two days time then. We've stashed the German in our safe house in the Wicklows so I can't come up tomorrow. Is that OK?' He replied, noting that Kelly had not asked him if he'd told the Chief of Staff.

'That'll be fine. You can stay with me overnight.' Said Kelly as he put the phone down.

Liam O'Donnell went to bed that night excited at the prospect of some real action and looking forward to working with his longterm mentor and friend. His only nagging doubt was the possibility that in the process he might be making an enemy of the Chief of Staff. The following day at 5am he bade his wife goodbye and headed south from Dublin deep into the Wicklow Mountains. His plan was to collect the German and immediately drive north up the middle of Ireland on minor roads all the way to Monaghan and an IRA safe house where they could spend the night. It would be a very long day but it would make the following day's drive into Belfast much easier. Crossing the border into Northern Ireland from Monaghan would be relatively straightforward as only the major roads had manned customs posts but having a German in the car increased the risk significantly. The local IRA would be able to give them directions on the safest route across the border to Armagh and from there he knew the route via Moira and Lisburn into Belfast. He reckoned they'd be arriving at Pearce Kelly's house mid-afternoon at the latest.

Declan met them at the door, 'That didn't take long Liam, what's the verdict?'

'We're going to take the German up to Belfast to meet with Pearse Kelly. He'll decide whether we're going to collaborate on the Harland and Wolff campaign or not. How has Fritz been behaving?' Said Liam, moving straight into the room where the German Military Attaché was handcuffed to the bed. He looked up nervously. 'No problem. I kept him handcuffed to the bed to be safe but I don't think he had the slightest intention of trying to escape.' Said Declan, as Liam was releasing the German.

'Come on Fritz, we're taking you to meet one of our Battalion Commanders in Belfast and it's a long drive. I'm not going to tie you up but believe me, if you give me any trouble whatsoever on the journey I won't hesitate to shoot you. Understood?' Questioned Liam.

'You will have no problem with me. This is what I want - to talk to someone in the IRA who has the authority to do a deal.' Said Karl, very relieved that for now he wasn't going to be interrogated, however he still feared for his life, if the IRA decided not to collaborate then he'd probably be executed. He'd seen too much.

'What about me?' Asked Declan.

'I'll drop you off at Naas and you can get a bus back to Dublin from there.' Replied Liam who was anxious to get away as soon as possible. 'Now let's get moving.'

It was a quiet drive as far as Naas but after Declan was dropped off the IRA man and the German Military Attaché were soon engaged in conversation. The first topic was how green and beautiful the countryside was, even during the winter but it didn't take long before that petered out and inevitably it was the war that consumed them for the remainder of the drive.

'Do you really think you can successfully invade Britain now - surely the best opportunity was immediately after the Dunkirk fiasco? What a German botch that was! Over three hundred thousand troops trapped on the beach and you let them all escape? I imagine Adolf wasn't too happy about that?' Taunted Liam with a quick glance across at his travelling companion.

'You'd hardly expect me to say anything but 'yes' Liam,' replied Karl, feeling more secure than he'd felt for some time. 'The bombing of London and the other major cities has been a success and it is expected that the British morale will collapse before long. They'll then throw out Churchill and sue for peace. In the meantime we will continue to savage the convoys from the United States with our U-boat wolf-packs.'

Changing tack Liam responded, 'Germany will be in trouble if the Americans enter the war to support their oldest ally. Let's face it they're already sending the British food and arms as fast as they can.'

'It is a risk despite their declared policy of neutrality. But Britain will be defeated before America can save them.' Said Karl who wasn't sure where Liam's loyalties lay. Perhaps he was simply keeping his options open, bearing in mind that everyone knew most of the IRA's funding was coming from the Irish communities in New England, principally Boston.

'What about Russia? Do you really think that the Molotov–Ribbentrop Pact will last? From where I stand it looks more like a political way of keeping Russia at bay while you rampage across Europe. Isn't the reality that Germans and Russians hate each other, right?' Said Liam, now having fun baiting the German. He continued without waiting for Karl's response, *'and why do you hate the Jews so much?'*

Karl had received no training in diplomacy prior to his appointment in the Dublin Embassy but this last remark made it obvious even to him that he was being baited and that trying to justify the Nazi anti-Semitism to an Irishman was probably a waste of time, so instead or answering Liam's questions he played the ball back to him, *'These are difficult times for the IRA, aren't they? I understand you are under intense pressure from your Government at the moment and that many of your members have been interned and it's been a long time since I read about the IRA doing anything significant either on the mainland or in the North of Ireland,'* he paused but continued before Liam could reply, *'Of course that's why I'm here. If we work together on this there's great potential for both of us, you will gain supply of arms and explosives and we will sink more British ships.'*

'That will not be up to me Karl. First we'll see how the Belfast Battalion Commander wants to play it but an operation like this will require the support of the IRA High Command.' Replied Liam as Karl noticed it had been a while since he'd been addressed as Fritz. A good sign he thought.

It was growing dark as they neared the outskirts of Monaghan. It had been a long day and both men were tired and hungry, however Liam was obliged to take the usual precautions before turning up at the safe house. They stopped at a telephone kiosk where Liam made a quick call to let his colleagues know they would be arriving shortly and to get any last minute instructions. There was always the chance that the safe house had been discovered by the Garda so it was routine practice to call ahead. Before introducing himself Liam spoke the password and on receiving the correct response he briefly confirmed he'd be there in a few minutes and that he would be accompanied by a German who wished to collaborate with them. He got the all-clear and shortly afterwards they rolled up in front of an innocuous semi-detached house in a quiet residential area on the northern edge of the town. The garage was open when they arrived so he drove straight in and five minutes later they were sitting around the kitchen table eating large helpings of Irish stew. Liam was careful not to go into any details about their mission but he had no need to emphasise its importance. With a German in tow it was obvious to him that the end result would be a much needed supply of arms and explosives.

'What's your plan now, Liam.' said their host.

Between mouthfuls he replied, 'we'll be off mid-morning to Belfast. I'd like to get there early afternoon. What are things like at the border?'

'Everybody is very jumpy at the moment, I don't know why but the British have increased their patrols recently and in the last couple of weeks there have been a number significant military exercises in the Armagh area. Crossing the border is still straightforward but there are new roadblocks and I'd say the chances are better than fifty-fifty you'll get stopped at least once between here and Belfast. The roadblocks aren't fixed either so basically you could be stopped anywhere.'

Liam stopped eating and looked across at his colleague, 'That's not good. My cover is OK but Karl here would be picked up immediately - his diplomatic immunity isn't much use in the UK.' He continued eating in silence for a while as Karl looked on, 'I'll have to phone Belfast and see if they can meet us here - would that be OK with you? Can you put us up for a couple of nights?'

'Should be fine - usual rules - you'll have to stay indoors and away from windows etcetera.' He responded helpfully, 'But I'll enjoy the company.'

Liam finished his stew, wiped his mouth and left the kitchen to make the telephone call to Pearce Kelly leaving Karl and the manager of the IRA safe-house to tidy up. It was some time before he returned.

'He'll be here tomorrow lunchtime,' he said, deliberately not mentioning his name. Pearce Kelly was a very important member of the IRA and would have been on the most-wanted list on both sides of the border, so the fewer people who knew his movements the better. Three bottles of Guinness were produced and shortly after they were finished Liam and Karl went to bed in a twin bedded room upstairs at the back of the house. As they lay in the dark Karl asked tentatively, *'Liam, would it be OK for me to call the German ambassador and at least let him know I'm safe?'*

'No,' said Liam emphatically, *'now go to sleep.'*

The ambassador was worried and it wasn't just Karl he was worrying about. It had been his responsibility to ensure that Karl was tailed and now he had both his boss, Ribbentrop, Admiral Dönitz and the Abwehr all asking for updates. A failure of this nature might not mean his removal as the German Ambassador to Ireland but it would certainly stain his hitherto unblemished record and probably limit his chances of promotion to one of the more senior ambassadorial roles. So he'd taken the risky decision to conceal the fact that he no longer had the slightest idea where Karl was or even if he was still alive. He was still hoping against hope that Karl would get in touch or he might receive an anonymous telephone call from the IRA to say he was being held but so far there had been only silence and as time went on, the likelihood that he'd have to confess to losing Karl was increasing sharply. He was already trying to concoct a story but it was going to be very difficult to explain how Karl had vanished. His last resort would be to try to make direct contact with the IRA but that was very risky indeed. If it ever became known to the Irish Government then there was absolutely no doubt his career as a German diplomat would be over and his future would be very dark indeed. The Third Reich did not look kindly on political embarrassment. His immediate dilemma was how best to time his feedback. If Karl was dead then the longer he left reporting back, the worse it would be for him but on the other hand he could appreciate the irony of admitting his failure to keep tabs on his military attaché and then within hours hearing from him. He felt sure that somehow his disappearance was connected with the Beggars Bush bar so he decided to pay a visit himself on the off-chance he could pick up some information. That evening after he'd eaten he walked around the the Beggars Bush and ordered a whiskey at the bar.

'Nice to see you again Mister Ambassador,' said Seamus the barman cheerfully, *'it's been a while since you last darkened our doorway.'*

'I beg your pardon? What do you mean? How have I darkened your door?' Replied Herr Lange, *'by the way you can call me Herman.'*

'I'm Seamus and it was just an expression which says it's been a long time since your shadow crossed our threshold - if you see what I mean? There was no threat or anything involved. You're very welcome!' Said Seamus who was feeling slightly flustered that his important customer might have got the wrong impression that he wasn't welcome. From previous experience the ambassador wasn't the easiest person to strike up a conversation with so he thought it best if he let Herman set the pace. For his part, Herman also felt a bit awkward and very uncertain about how to pursue his mission to find out what had happened to Karl. Fortunately Seamus came to his rescue and asked how he felt the war was going. This was home territory for the ambassador who skilfully summed up the status without giving away anything. He needed to be careful because he had no way of knowing if Seamus was an IRA sympathiser or even an agent for the Directorate of Military Intelligence, the G2 and if neither, he didn't even know where his loyalties lay. For his part, Seamus was also an expert in steering a middle path so for an hour and several further whiskeys they did the conversational equivalent of a pavement tango, each superficially confiding in the other but neither saying anything of substance. It soon became obvious to both of them that the ambassador hadn't come to the Beggars Bush to shoot the breeze with the barman. There must be a hidden agenda. His tongue loosened by several large Jamesons, the ambassador glanced furtively around the bar to make sure nobody was within earshot and then leaning forward across the counter he said softly and with the slightest hint of a slur, *'Seamus, have you seen Karl Wagner in here recently?'*

For a few seconds the barman looked questioningly at him and then shaking his head slightly from side to side he replied. *'Karl who?'*

To the ambassador it felt like a bucket of ice-cold water had been poured over his head. It was obvious he had stepped over a line with his enquiry. *'He works at the embassy and I seem to remember him saying that you serve an excellent pint of Guinness here.'* He said unconvincingly while climbing off his barstool and preparing to leave, *'Well Seamus, I must be off now. It was a pleasure meeting you.'* And resisting the usual instinctive reaction to click his heels he left the pub with his head swirling. He'd learnt precisely nothing about the fate of his military attaché and indirectly he'd told the barman that Karl was missing. It was definitely not his finest hour. By the time he got home he'd decided all he could do was wait and see if Karl got in touch but if the silence continued for much longer his career as a diplomat was exposed. Losing the military attaché was probably something he could have survived but concealing the fact that he had lost him was not.

In the safe house in Monaghan Liam and Karl passed the morning with a leisurely fry-up breakfast and several mugs of tea while they waited for Pearse Kelly to arrive. Apart from the usual pleasantries the conversation between them was very limited. They had nothing in common other than their shared enemy but although technically that made them friends, in reality that was only a convenience. In any event Liam was engrossed with the problem of how the sabotage plan could be put in place. He wanted to be able to contribute to the discussion with Pearse and thereby ensure his continued involvement. Whoever was assigned the task of sabotaging the corvette production line in the Harland and Wolff shipyard would be an IRA hero if he pulled it off and a martyr if he failed. Despite the risks he knew he'd jump at the chance if it came his way.

Shortly after noon a car rolled up outside the house where it stopped briefly to drop off the Belfast Battalion Commander and then immediately sped away. Liam rushed to meet him at the door where he ushered him inside and helped him off with his coat and scarf. As he removed Pearse's scarf he got a shock. Underneath it the Battalion Commander was wearing a dog collar. *'Jazus Pearse, so you're a priest now?'* he said, his face filling with a broad smile.

'Good to see you again Liam, how about you put the kettle on for a brew and I'll explain, but our top priority is to decide how to handle the proposition from the Germans. We have a lot to discuss and only when we've finished do I want to meet him, OK?' Said Pearse authoritatively as he headed for the kitchen and his mug of tea. As they waited for the

kettle to boil he explained the dog collar. *'A while back we discovered that the bishop was a homosexual, something he was rather keen to keep secret. Now you know we like to keep the church onside but this nugget presented us with a golden opportunity. When I suggested to him that I might become a lay priest in his diocese he was happy to appoint me on the spot and here I am - a Catholic priest. So if you want to confess anything, I'm yer mon!'* He chuckled, speaking with an exaggerated Ulster accent, *'it's the perfect cover. The police will always think twice before upsetting the Catholic church, even though they know where their sympathies lie.'*

'Nice one Pearse, can you do miracles?' Said Liam enjoying the banter.

'Sadly no, but let's get down to business, tell me about this potential collaboration with the Germans.' He said with a tone which indicated the banter was over.

For more than an hour the two IRA men were immersed in deep conversation about the idea of sabotaging the Harland and Wolff production line. Before there could be any dialogue with the Germans it was essential that this was a viable undertaking for the embattled IRA.

'The more credible a plan we put to the Germans the more arms we can ask them for. The legitimacy of our claim is completely dependent on how realistic a plan we can put before them. We need to be convinced we can pull this off and go to the negotiating table armed with this knowledge. So, instead of concentrating on what we might ask from Herr Hitler in return, we need to come up with a plan which we think will work. Only then is it worthwhile embarking on negotiations and even then, they'd be mugs to agree up front to anything more than a percentage of what we're asking. The final payment will be conditional on us delivering the plan.' Said Pearse.

'Are you thinking of running this as an entirely Northern Irish operation without taking direction from the High Command?' Queried Liam.

'You're getting distracted again, Liam,' responded Pearse, *'what you and I need to work on is how we can pull this off. So, have you any ideas?'*

'Personally I don't think it could be done without inside help. Do you have any sleepers in Harland and Wolff?'

'No, we don't. You probably know that they only employ Protestants which doesn't make it an easy company to infiltrate. Let's assume for the minute that we can enlist an employee who works on the corvette production line, he'd have to be trained in explosives - German explosives - and then somehow we've got to find out where to put them in order to maximise the disruption...' He paused as he thought about that for a minute, 'we're going to need some expert advice on where to place the explosives. Maybe we should find this out first because whoever we get to work in the yard will have to be employed in a part of the process where he can legitimately access these critical locations? I'm beginning to think that we'll need more than one person inside Harland and Wolff if we're going to pull this off.' He sighed and stood up. 'Time for another brew. This isn't going to be easy but it is a golden opportunity to rearm and continue the struggle to get the Brits out of Ireland. If this succeeds it will have a huge positive impact on our morale. Let's face it, we've been on the back foot since the war started.'

Liam was impressed with the Pearse's intensity and apparent determination to exploit this opportunity to the full and he felt privileged to be involved. For a while he flirted with the idea that he might be selected for the job but he quickly realised that for a variety reasons he was far from the ideal choice. First, he was a Catholic and although by no means devout, he knew that when surrounded by Protestants day in day out, sooner or later he would give himself away and second, he had a thick Irish brogue which would instantly brand him as being from the South. In a way he was relieved. The man who took on this job would run a high risk of becoming an IRA martyr and as a family man this wasn't something he relished although when he'd taken the oath of allegiance he pledged to give his life for the cause if called to do so. This seemed natural at the time, after all they were at war. The IRA had made a formal declaration of war on the British on the 12th of January 1939 in a letter to Viscount Halifax, the British Foreign Secretary and three days later, it having been ignored, a proclamation was posted in public places throughout Ireland announcing that the IRA was at war with Britain. There'd been rumours at the time that the decision by the IRA's Army Council hadn't been unanimous and that one of the seven members, Máirtín Ó Cadhain, had refused to sign the letter because he felt that the IRA wasn't ready. It had been a heady time and on the back of it recruitment surged briefly, however it soon became apparent within the ranks that the declaration of war was seen more as 'grand gesture' than the launching of a serious campaign to rid Ireland of the British because it was obvious that the IRA had neither the arms nor the explosives to effect a bombing campaign at that time. After the invasion of Poland when Britain declared war on Germany an opportunity to collaborate with the Germans had arisen and since then there'd been numerous attempts to secure a supply of arms from the Nazis. So far these had only been partially successful but this opportunity could change all that. Like most grass-roots members of the IRA, Máirtín Ó Cadhain was much admired for his love of the Irish language and for his many literary works. Liam wondered if he rued the memorable oration he gave at the funeral of his friend Tony Darcy who died on hunger strike in Mountjoy Prison seeking political prisoner status. Ó Cadhain was now in the Curragh, having been arrested shortly afterwards.

They finished their brew in silence and then Pearse announced decisively, *'Liam, we're off to Dublin first thing in the morning. You tell him. I would like to remain anonymous to him so don't address me by name in his presence - just call me Father. The fewer people who know who I am the better. Diplomatic immunity or not, if the Directorate got a whiff of us collaborating with the Germans and picked Fritz up they'd soon be on our trail. I'll sit in the back seat of the car and as far as he's concerned I'm just a priest who's getting a lift to Dublin - OK?'*

'Got it.' Said Liam before leaving the room to brief Karl who wasn't overjoyed about being kept in the dark but nonetheless understood the IRA's need for caution. *'We'll be on our way back to Dublin tomorrow and we'll be leaving before dawn so you might want to get an early night.'*

'Does this mean the operation is going ahead?' Enquired Karl hopefully.

'Karl, the operation is still under consideration - otherwise why would we bother keeping you alive?' Said Liam, immediately regretting his pointlessly aggressive tone.

The next morning in the early greyness of the dawn the three men set off on the long drive to Dublin. Liam drove and as arranged Karl was beside him in the passenger seat and the Belfast Battalion Commander sat alone in the back seat. They drove in silence for most of the way. From time to time Karl wondered why the priest was travelling with them but he considered it unwise to ask questions. Since his abduction he'd become aware of just how stressful being a member of the IRA was. The merciless aggression being pursued by the Irish Government against the organisation was straining it to the limit and had created an atmosphere of suspicion and intrigue which was now part of everyday life for the dwindling number of members who remained dedicated to the cause. It was clear that working with the IRA was going to require extreme care and the utmost tact but he was becoming increasingly optimistic that a deal was possible. He resolved only to speak when he was spoken to but his suspicions about the mysterious priest in the back seat continued to fester.

Patrick McGonigle was a happy man. Since he'd started working at the Irish Steam Packet Company his life was back on track again after losing his job in Donegal and moving to Dublin. His skill as a welder had quickly been recognised by the foreman and although his basic wage wasn't spectacular he was already getting lots of overtime. At the Beggars Bush he was now part of the scene and on first name terms with most of the regulars. He'd realised there was an unofficial but nevertheless quite organised structure to the pub society. Most everyone was in a rut. They sat in the same seat or at the same table, they ordered the same drink, *'the usual'*, they arrived and left at the same times and their conversation always followed the same pattern - *'How's the missus? Is your back any better? I'm fed up with this weather,'* and so on. Each regular had his own comfort zone and although they overlapped to some degree there were long-established cliques. It was his job to understand all this and to fit into the overall society of the pub. At first sight his job was as mundane as they came but like so many regulars in pubs across the length and breadth of Ireland he realised that this society was the core of his social life. Of course like all Irishmen, the great issues of life were thoroughly explored but there were no-go areas and since he'd started working at the Beggars Bush he had never overheard any discussion about the IRA.

But the absence of any talk about the IRA had begun to make him suspicious. There was also one group of five which assembled twice a week and although they were clearly 'regulars' in every sense of the word they always sat in a booth at the far end of the bar which by its location was more private than anywhere else in the pub. When he served them drinks he noticed that the conversation which had been intense as he carried the tray of Guinness to the booth always dried up completely when he arrived. That's not say they were impolite - quite the reverse. Everyone in the pub knew he had got a job at the Irish Steam Packet Company and they were forever asking him *'How's it going Patrick?'* He didn't even know Mick's second name but unofficially or otherwise, it was easy to see that he was in charge. The other thing he noticed was that when the pub was quiet his employer Seamus would occasionally join Mick's group. It was probably perfectly normal as Mick's twice weekly gatherings were as predictable as the tides so the line between customer and friend had naturally become blurred. However Patrick was coming to the conclusion that there was more to this group than met the eye and he began to wonder if perhaps they were IRA sympathisers or maybe even members. His curiosity ate away at him but such were the conditions in the IRA at that time it would be dangerous for him to directly enquire. If he asked around and they heard about it, their assumption might be that he was a government agent in which case he could easily end up in the Liffey. Another approach would be to give off signals that he was an IRA sympathiser but that also might lead them to conclude he was a spy. And what if they had nothing to do with the IRA? It was rumoured that passing on the names of IRA members to the Directorate of Military Intelligence was worth ten punts and even if that was done anonymously, it would be taking a huge risk. It was common knowledge that if the IRA ever found out who had betrayed them they would be in for a very painful death. Not that he would have the slightest inclination to betray them but if by some other means they were investigated, it could easily be assumed that he was the source. He then wondered how he would respond if they asked him about his views on the struggle for a united Ireland which was generally accepted as a coded way of enquiring whether someone was an IRA sympathiser or not. It made him smile when he remembered how a similar coded question in the North was used to determine whether someone was a Catholic or a Protestant. *'What school did you go to?'* might sound like an innocent question but in a segregated education system, if the title of the school you went to contained the word 'Saint' then it was a fair assumption that you were a Catholic. He had no pressing need to know if the Beggars Bush was an IRA pub or not so he continued to avoid any discussion which might give away the fact that he was a member. A while back an American from the US Embassy had been in the pub and used the expression, *'The elephant in the room'*. It struck him how appropriate it was in the Beggars Bush, the IRA was the elephant in the room - everybody knew it was there but nobody was prepared to talk about it.

Then one evening everything changed. He was serving behind the bar with Seamus one Friday night when a priest and another man entered the pub. They went directly up to Seamus who immediately ushered them through the door at the back which led to the upstairs accommodation. As he left he said, *'bring three pints of Guinness upstairs to the sitting room Patrick, we have some thirsty visitors.'* Patrick poured the three drinks, set them on a tray and carried them carefully upstairs to where Seamus and his two visitors were immersed in deep conversation. As he entered they pointedly stopped talking and Seamus said, *'Thanks Pat, I need you to look after the bar for a while. Please ask Mick to join us and after that make sure that we're not disturbed.'*

'No problem.' He replied, directly leaving the room and heading back downstairs to tend the bar. There was now no doubt in his mind that what he'd left was an IRA meeting and it was equally obvious that what he had begun to suspect was true, both Seamus and Mick were important players. It was a very busy hour for Patrick looking after the bar on his own before Seamus and Mick reappeared. Mick resumed his usual place in the far booth with his mates and Seamus began pulling pints without a word while the trio in the corner belted out a rebel number to the delight of the sing-along crowd. Shortly afterwards one of other men came downstairs and swiftly left the pub leaving the priest upstairs on his own.

It was late and Karl was mightily relieved as he strode quickly down Haddington Road on the five minute walk back to the German Embassy. Turning left into Northumberland Road he couldn't help glancing back towards the pub to see if he was being tailed, quickly realising that would have been highly unlikely, the IRA had let him go specifically so he could return to the Embassy and set the wheels in motion for the collaboration. It had been a scary few days but in the end he'd accomplished his task so it was a smiling Military Attaché which was ushered into the ambassador's office. The door had barely closed behind him before the ambassador jumped to his feet and walked around his desk with his hand outstretched, *'Karl, you've no idea how pleased I am to see you!'* he said as he warmly shook Karl's hand, *'we've been desperately worried.'* Karl was touched by the ambassador's obvious relief that he had returned in one piece, little realising that the ambassador's relief was mostly because only minutes earlier he'd decided to make the call to Ribbentrop in the morning and admit his failure to keep tabs on the Military Attaché. *'Is the operation going to go ahead?'* he questioned urgently.

In the next hour Karl told his story to the ambassador who interrupted from time to time with questions. He explained that it was far from a done deal yet but without going into details the IRA seemed to think they could pull it off. However they had presented him with some demands which they wanted met before agreeing to take the project to the IRA High Command for approval.

'Tell me these demands. We can discuss them with Ribbentrop tomorrow.' he queried at which point Karl handed a piece of paper to the ambassador. His eyes widened as he read it, *'This is an enormous quantity of arms - are they planning to invade the North?'* he joked, *'even if this is agreed it will be a major job to deliver these guns and explosives safely.'*

'We didn't discuss that Herr Lange,' said Karl, *'They want you and me to meet them again in two days time when they will go into more detail about how they intend to sabotage the corvette production line in Harland and Wolff. They will telephone you personally with the time and place of the meeting. They didn't say when they were going to call but*

they did emphasise that we needed to get agreement to the arms shipment tomorrow and be ready to talk the following day.'

Herman Lange breathed a long sigh of relief. *'Well done Karl, let's have a small drink to celebrate your safe return and the beginning of our collaboration with the IRA. You'll be happy to sleep in your own bed tonight!'* He poured two glasses of schnapps and handed one to Karl, *'Let's drink a toast to Operation Harland and Wolff.'* They clinked glasses and downed their drinks. *'Heil Hitler,'* said Karl as he clicked his heels and bade the ambassador goodnight. He was suddenly exhausted having been living on his nerves since the moment he'd been abducted. He'd done his job and it was the ambassador who now had the ball. Less than a half hour later he had showered and was climbing into his bed, totally drained but still wondering who the priest was and what position he held in the IRA.

Early the following morning Herman Lange called Joachim von Ribbentrop in Berlin and when the connection was made he stood up to make the call. It was an automatic reaction when speaking to his boss, the German Foreign Minister and Hitler's top diplomat since 1933. There were rumours that Ribbentrop wasn't the brightest of the senior Nazis but being a favourite of Hitler's ensured his longevity in the job. It had been Ribbentrop who had personally appointed him as the German Ambassador to Ireland and it would be Ribbentrop who would decide his future when his term in Ireland was over. He was enjoying his assignment but until now he had been relatively invisible, this collaboration with the IRA was the perfect opportunity for him to impress Ribbentrop and further his career in the German Foreign Service. When the call was put through, Ribbentrop picked up the phone and said, *'Herman, how are you? I was wondering when you were going to call. I was beginning to think things might not be going well over there.'*

'On the contrary Sir, we have made contact with the IRA and we have their provisional agreement to proceed with the collaboration. They will carry out the operation at Harland and Wolff in exchange for arms and explosives. I have a list of their demands and we need to agree to them before we can go any further.' Said Herman holding at the ready the piece of paper containing the full list of the IRA demands.

There was a pause before Ribbentrop responded impatiently, *'well, go on then - tell me their demands.'* Herman read the list to him and when he'd finished he wasn't sure if the line had dropped because there was a very long pause. Then Ribbentrop spoke in a voice no longer jovial and relaxed, *'That is ridiculous! There's enough equipment there to arm a complete division - are you sure they don't want any tanks as well?'*

Now on the defensive Herman responded carefully, *'I agree their demands are outrageous but we've not even started to negotiate. I'm sure that we can reach a mutually acceptable agreement with the IRA but it will be a step-by-step process. We've still not seen their plan and of course before we agree to anything we've got to know that it's been thought through and has a reasonable chance of success.'*

'Reasonable! Not a word I would apply to this demand but I suppose you're right.' Ribbentrop harrumphed down the phone line. *'Clearly you need to meet with them again and reset their expectations but Dönitz has been onto me asking if any progress has been made. Meet with them, agree in principle that we will supply them with munitions and get back to me as soon as possible. In the meantime if Dönitz calls again, I will make sure he knows it will be his job to find the arms and to deliver them - this is far too big a shipment to be delivered by air. Call me immediately after your meeting - OK?'*

'Yes Herr Ribbentrop, of course.' He replied, gratefully hearing the click from the other end of the line which signalled that the Foreign Minister had hung up. *'Get Wagner in here now,'* he barked into the speaker phone which connected him to his secretary, *'bring some coffee and biscuits and make sure they are pfeffernüsses.*

After their meeting Karl called Seamus, the barman at the Beggars Bush and arranged to meet them at the pub immediately after lunch when the bar was at its quietest. On arrival they were ushered directly to the upstairs room where Liam, Mick and the priest were sitting behind the table. Seamus gestured to the facing seats and then returned to the bar leaving the four men alone together. After the introductions were made the priest who had been introduced simply as 'father' opened the discussion by asking if their demands for armaments would be met. Trying not to sound too defensive, the ambassador replied, *'In principle*

- yes. I have the commitment of Herr Ribbentrop himself that we are prepared to supply you with arms and explosives in return for sabotaging the corvette production line at Harland and Wolff but we'd like to see an outline of your plan before take your demand any further.'

The three IRA men exchanged glanced and then the priest spoke, making it abundantly clear to the Germans that he was the senior officer. *'I am the Battalion Commander for the IRA in Belfast and the High Command has agreed that this will be my operation.'* It was a blatant lie because the IRA trio knew that for security reasons they had deliberately chosen not to consult the High Command at this stage. The option remained open but for the time being it was felt that the fewer people who knew of this plan the better. He then went on to outline in principle how the operation would be carried out. *'We will plant one or maybe two of our members in Harland and Wolff as employees working on the production line. Once their positions are secure they will assemble a cache of explosives over a period of days until there is enough to cause major damage to as many ships as possible. Both men will need training on the use of German plastic explosives and whether you do that in Ireland with one of your agents or in Germany is up to you. The former will undoubtedly be quicker but be warned the lead-time on this operation will be a minimum of three months and more likely five months. Now let's talk about the armaments.'*

The Ambassador cleared his throat, glanced across at Karl and then responded, *'As I already said, we are fully prepared to provide arms and explosives to support this operation...'* but he was unable to finish his sentence when the the priest pointedly slapped the table and interrupted, *'Hang on a minute Herman, the arms and explosives we're demanding aren't only those to support this operation. We want to re-arm the IRA so we can continue our struggle for a united Ireland. If this operation is as important to Germany as you've implied, then it's a bargain for you, much cheaper and more effective than a bombing raid.'*

There was a lengthy silence before the ambassador spoke again, *'Poor choice of words on my part, I'm sorry, I think we understand this Father and I hope we can reach agreement on the size of the arms shipment but I think that negotiation would be easier if we first agreed on the principle of half the arms before the operation and the other half once it's been successfully completed?'*

'If you agree on the total, then we agree on splitting it half before and half after.' Said the priest, now in full negotiating mode.

'I do not have the authority to say yes on this but I'm prepared to put the question to my superiors and get back to you. It would help if you were able to identify your men for the job so we can arrange for them to be trained on our explosives.' Said the ambassador, wanting to have as much as possible to present to Ribbentrop in their next telephone. He'd already decided that horse-trading on the size of shipment was going to be difficult. increasing the risk of both delaying the operation and creating bad feeling between them and the IRA. Although the quantity of arms they were seeking was excessive, it was insignificant in the overall scheme of things to the Germany military.

'We'll select the men while you talk to your superiors. The sooner we see the first shipment, the sooner we can get this operation underway.' Said the priest, clearly indicating to the Germans that the ball was in their court. During the next hour they talked about the detailed logistics of the arms shipment on the assumption that it was going to go ahead. It was agreed that an airdrop was too risky so the arms would have to be brought in by boat, either a trawler or a submarine. The priest insisted that the shipment should be brought into Northern Ireland as it was the Belfast Brigade that was running the operation. His preferred option was Lough Foyle, a large sheltered expanse of water with the border running down the centre of it. Irish fishing boats based in Moville or Greencastle regularly came and went into the North Atlantic through the narrows at the mouth of the lough, passing within shouting distance of the British fortifications on Magilligan Point. Once inside the Lough a small boat could easily land the arms anywhere on the Northern Irish shoreline but because it was very shallow this would only be possible within an hour either side of full tide. Londonderry, the second largest city in the province had a large community which supported the republican cause and so the manpower required to shift the munitions to one or more secret dumps would be readily available. The Germans made copious notes and before the meeting broke up they were reminded by the priest that the IRA needed a firm commitment on the

arms shipment before they would do anything more than identify the men who would carry out the operation. After that they bluntly stated that it wouldn't be kicked off until the arms were safely in the hands of the IRA. At this the ambassador protested, *'This will delay the schedule, you don't need the explosives until your men are safely established inside Harland and Wolff and that will take weeks, possibly months.'*

'Take it or leave it,' replied the priest, *'and another thing, you will need to send an explosives expert with the first shipment. Our men can be trained as part of that exercise, they are already experienced and fast learners so it shouldn't take more than a couple of hours. You can either do that on the ship you send with the arms or in Greencastle where we have a safe house. Also, during the operation we will need your Attaché's presence in Belfast.'*

Karl looked nervously at his boss but said nothing. He could see that it made sense from both the German and the IRA's standpoint but he also quickly realised that he would effectively be a hostage. If there were any hiccups with the second shipment of arms he would be the IRA's bargaining chip and there was the added concern that he would be spending several months in enemy territory.

'I agree. Once your men are safely established as employees at Harland and Wolff, Karl will join your team in Belfast and handle all the communications with Germany.' Said the ambassador, pointedly not even glancing at his colleague who was already resigning himself to the prospect of a very dangerous few months. There would be no easy path to promotion for him, he sighed to himself.

During the following few days things happened fast. The German U-Boats were doing terrible damage to the North Atlantic convoys and the British losses were mounting. Admiral Dönitz was charged by Hitler to starve Britain into submission and it was crucial to the German cause that these convoys remained as unprotected as possible. Every new escort naval vessel whether a destroyer, frigate or corvette that was built made his job more difficult. They were in a deadly race, Germany was building U-boats as fast as possible and Britain was building escort vessels to defend the convoys equally fast. The next few months were critical. Currently he had his jackboot on Britain's neck and now he wanted to finish the job. When Ribbentrop forwarded the IRA's demands to him Dönitz barely read them before he phoned the Foreign Minister and barked down the phone, *'Well what are you waiting for - let's get moving.'* They went on to discuss the logistics and agreed that Dönitz would load the munitions onto a U-boat and divert it around the North of Ireland to rendezvous with an IRA fishing boat which could land the arms somewhere in Donegal, ideally inside Lough Foyle at either Greencastle or Moville. In the meantime Dönitz pressed his colleague to stress the urgency to the IRA and do everything within his power to help them sabotage the Harland and Wolff shipyard. *'I want a weekly report Joachim. Call me personally. This is a top priority. We are winning the battle of the Atlantic and total defeat of the British is within our grasp. Heil Hitler!'*

Oblivious to all this Patrick McGonigle was enjoying life. His work at the Irish Steam Packet Company was going well and his star was rising. The management had quickly noticed the quality of his work and placed him in a group of elite welders who were given the most challenging jobs and in the Beggars Bush he had become part of the establishment, often running the bar on his own when Seamus was attending to other business. He'd noticed the goings-on with the priest and assumed that it was IRA work but he hadn't enquired. He had no reason to disclose his membership of the IRA and no-one had asked him about it so he kept his head down and hoped that the organisation had forgotten about him. At the same time he understood that joining the IRA meant he was in it for life and traditionally the only way to leave was in a coffin. Then one evening in the bar Seamus said, *'Patrick, there's something I want to talk to you about. Can you stay behind after closing time?'*

'No problem Seamus.' He replied, fearing that something was afoot.

They tidied up the bar after the last of the regulars had left and then retired to the upstairs room where Seamus took the seat behind the table and gestured to towards the seat on the opposite side of the table. Even before Seamus opened his mouth he knew what was coming.

'Patrick, we've known since you arrived in Dublin that you were a member of the IRA and I'm happy to be able to tell you that we've got a job for you - one for which you are uniquely qualified. We have the

opportunity to collaborate with the Germans in an operation at the Harland and Wolff shipyard. They want us to sabotage the production of naval escort vessels in the shipyard in exchange for a massive shipment of guns and explosives which will keep us armed for the foreseeable future.'

'Uniquely qualified?' Queried Patrick.

'Yes,' said Seamus, 'you are a skilled welder and you are also a Protestant. You probably know that Harland and Wolff is notorious for only employing Proddies so you shouldn't have any problems getting a job with them and they need good welders as they are trying to ramp up production.'

'You want me to get a job working at Harland and Wolff?' asked Patrick, feeling that his world was about to fall apart. When he was in Buncrana he had longed for some meaningful action but since he'd moved to Dublin and settled down into his new life he'd become much less passionate about the reunification of Ireland. However, he could squirm as much as he liked but he knew that the IRA didn't make requests, they issued orders and Seamus was giving him an order.

'Yes Patrick, we need you to get a job working in the shipyard as a welder so you can have unrestricted access to the ships. The Germans will train you how to use their plastic explosives and you will lay these explosives where they will do the maximum amount of damage. If you do this right, you won't necessarily be suspected but if you are rumbled we will bale you out and see you are spirited out of the province. What do you say?' Said Seamus, pausing to let him respond.

Biting his lip he replied with fake enthusiasm, 'Sounds massive. Obviously I've lots of questions but what about my job at the Irish Steam Packet Company?'

'We've had a word with our friends there and they are more than happy to release you for this important mission and they've promised to hold the job open for you once it's complete. Our estimate is that the operation shouldn't take more than three months start to finish. We will pay the rent on your flat so it will be here for you when you return.'

'When do I start?' He enquired, now resigned to his fate but aware of a faint tingle of excitement. This was obviously a massive operation and with him in the key role it was just what he'd have wanted a few months ago, but no longer. He'd only just settled down in Dublin and he was less than enthusiastic about leaving all that behind.

'You start immediately. The operation will be run by the Belfast Brigade and we've organised transport to take you up there tomorrow. You've no need to go into work at the Steam Packet Company again until the operation is over. They are not expecting to see you for at least three months. Pack what you need and Mick and Liam will drive you to Belfast. Oh by the way there will be one other passenger, the German Military Attaché, Karl Wagner. He'll be handling liaison with the Germans and he is also our insurance policy to make sure they keep their side of the bargain. Ok, Patrick, that's enough for now. I know it's late but let's have one for the road.' Seamus stood up, reached across the table and shook Patrick's hand warmly, 'You're a good man Patrick McGonigle, this is the biggest IRA operation in my lifetime and there's many a man who would give anything to have the opportunity you have to go down in the annals as one of the great Irish patriots.' he said as he led the way downstairs and poured them each a glass of the finest Irish whiskey in the bar, a rare bottle of Midleton. They downed the whiskey, said their goodbyes and went their separate ways, Patrick's head spinning with thoughts of what lay ahead. He knew this would be a very dangerous mission and there would be a good chance he might die but if he did, he knew he would die a hero and be remembered for ever.

The drive north was uneventful and on reaching Monaghan they holed up in the safe house awaiting intelligence on where they should cross the border into Northern Ireland. The main roads had controlled checkpoints manned by customs officials and the army and these were to be avoided at all costs. The remainder of the more than two hundred and fifty minor roads that crossed the border were patrolled by the British army on a random basis. This surveillance activity was continually monitored by IRA 'observers' who could then reliably predict which roads were the safest to use on any particular day but the presence of the German military attaché in the car significantly increased the risk. Ordinarily the other two IRA men had cover stories which would have sufficed but having Karl with them would guarantee internment for all three. However it was clear they had no choice but to have him as part of the team, at least until the arms shipments were complete. Early the following morning when they received the information on the safest crossing point they left immediately and with some relief crossed undetected into Northern Ireland. A couple of hours later they arrived at the Belfast Battalion Commander's home on the Falls Road where they were warmly greeted by Pearse Kelly, no longer in his guise as a Catholic priest. There was a buzz in the air as they sat down to talk over the plans for the operation. This was a major project against the British and it also promised munitions which would keep the IRA supplied for years ahead. Karl was immediately instructed to telephone the German embassy in Dublin, first to report his safe arrive in Belfast and then to find out when and where the first shipment of arms would be delivered, leaving the four IRA men together in the room. Obviously excited and highly motivated Pearse opened the meeting, *'Very glad you got here safely gents, we're definitely seeing an increase in activity from the British Army and we're pretty sure that they've stepped up undercover operations so we will have to be extra careful. Patrick, you're the main man now and we've put together a cover story. You're moving up to Belfast from Dublin to get married to your girlfriend Anne Docherty, who lives on Sandy Row with her mother, both of which are - surprise, surprise - Protestants but also undercover supporters of the cause. Anne and her mother Grace have both been briefed that this is a sabotage operation at Harland and Wolff but they don't know we're collaborating with the Germans and that there is a substantial arms shipment as part of the deal. Tomorrow you will make your way to their house on the bus. It would be too dangerous for me to take you and most certainly not disguised as a priest - I don't think I'd last long on Sandy Row wearing my dog-collar!'* They all laughed at the thought of a Priest dropping someone off at a house on Sandy Row, the most loyal of loyalist streets in Belfast. Pearse continued, *'The following day Patrick, you head over to Harland and Wolff and ask for a job. It's only a short distance so you can walk and there and maybe meet up with some other shipyard workers on the way. Our friend the boss of the Steam Packet Company has been briefed to expect a call from Harland and Wolff to check your credentials and he will give you a glowing report. You shouldn't have any problems but you will need to keep well away from any politics and especially avoid engaging in any way with the protestant paramilitary who we believe are recruiting in the shipyard. We have obtained a copy of your birth certificate for you and it records your religion. They will definitely want to see that.'*

Just then Karl returned having obtained details of how the first shipment of arms was to be delivered. The plan was for a U-boat to transport the arms west-about around Ireland, past Malin Head and down the northeast shore of Donegal where they could be transferred to a local Irish fishing boat somewhere off Culdaff. The trawler would transport them to Greencastle and from there, when the time was right, they would be transferred in several batches across Loch Foyle into Northern Ireland and hidden in an IRA arms cache near the village of Ballyscullion. *'While the arms are being transferred to the fishing boat Patrick, you will be given some basic tuition on how to handle the German plastic explosive. My understanding is that it's more or less the same as gelignite but they tell me it is more concentrated and it also smells differently - of almonds I believe! Our explosives people insist on you getting some training.'* Said Karl.

'That's fair enough,' responded Pearse, *'so you'll need a few days leave, Pat. We'll set up some cover story - death in the family or something.'*

'What about timing?' Enquired Liam.

'The agreement with the Germans is that we get half the arms before the operation and half when it's complete. They know we have no explosives so it's obvious they have to honour the deal. Our top priority is to secure the arms shipment and the Germans' top priority is to sabotage the corvette production line at Harland and Wolff. It's a good deal for both sides. Karl will ensure they keep to their commitment to send the second batch of arms.' Said Pearse, glancing pointedly across at the Military Attaché who was well aware of the fact that he wasn't only their liaison with the Germans, he was also their hostage.

'The date for the arms shipment has not been set. My superiors want to know that Patrick is established as an employee at Harland and Wolff beforehand.' Said Karl somewhat tentatively because embedded in his comment was an element of distrust. Pease exchanged a glance with Liam before responding, *'I suppose that's reasonable. If you get rumbled Patrick, then there is no plan B.'*

The following day Patrick made his way to Sandy Row to meet his arranged fiancée. He tried not to let his discomfort show as he walked from the bus stop to the house where she and her mother lived. He had a lot to be nervous about. As a member of the IRA he could not have been in a more dangerous place, even a whiff of his mission would guarantee a very painful death. He was also embarking on a perilous mission to sabotage the Harland and Wolff shipyard and whether it succeeded or failed depended entirely on him and finally, he was about to meet a girl he'd never seen before yet who was now his fiancée. Arriving at the house he saw an upstairs net curtain twitch and he felt sure someone had been watching for his arrival. Not sure what to expect he knocked tentatively at the door. A moment later it was flung open and he was emotionally embraced by an attractive young girl on the threshold in full view of anyone who happened to be watching, *'Patrick! It's been too long.'* She said, kissing him full on the lips. *'Come inside and make yourself at home.'*

Still reeling from their encounter on the doorstep with his arranged fiancée they went through to the kitchen where her mother was in the process of pouring out the tea, *'You must be Anne,'* he said, stating the blindingly obvious but for the moment unable to think of anything else to say.

'Nice to meet you Patrick.' She replied, flashing smile at him, *'This is my mother Grace.'*

He nodded towards her and held out his hand, *'Pleased to meet you Grace and thank you for your help.'* They shook hands warmly before he turned again to Anne, now feeling a little more in control, *'and what if I'd been a delivery boy or I'd come to read the meter or something?'* he enquired searchingly, *'I presume you don't greet all your visitors the same way?'*

'Only special visitors like you!' She replied and already he could feel the blossoming chemistry between them. He certainly felt attracted to her and it seemed that the feeling was mutual.

'You're in Sandy Row, Patrick. This is the lion's den and we need to be very careful to appear genuine at all times. New arrivals here are few and far between and are always greeted with suspicion. As soon as we heard you were coming we let the word out that you're my fiancée and

you're arriving today so you can be certain that at least half the street will have watched your arrival from behind their net curtains and by the time the men get back from the shipyard everyone will know my fiancée has arrived. This has all been quite sudden so it's only natural that our neighbours will be curious about you - even suspicious. We need to make sure that we tell the exactly the same story. Most of the shipyard workers are regulars at McHughs Bar in Queens Square and as soon as you're established you'll go there and you can be sure you'll get grilled by our neighbours all of whom work at Harland and Wolff. On Saturday nights we'll have to go to McHughs together.' She spoke with impressive assurance for someone who was so young but he knew she'd been through a harrowing experience when her father was brutally murdered as a suspected informer two years previously. Since then she'd been an IRA sympathiser constantly living with the risk of discovery and its terrible consequences. She may have been only twenty-two but she'd already seen much more of life and the troubles than he had. He would have to learn quickly because one false step could spell the end of the operation and be fatal for both of them. The enormity of his undertaking was beginning to come home to him and he felt weighed down by the responsibility.

That evening after dinner they talked late into the night. Initially it was about the project but as time went on their conversation became more personal. He wanted to understand the circumstances which led up to her switch in allegiance but he didn't like to probe. Eventually she described how her father, a loyalist to the core as far as she and her mother were concerned, had been suspected by the senior members of the local Orange Lodge of colluding with the IRA. She had no idea what he'd done to attract this attention but in the febrile atmosphere of Catholic/Protestant relations it quickly spiralled out of control and after being tried by a kangaroo court he was executed in the family home, more or less where Patrick was then sitting. Anne didn't even know if her father had ever participated in any terrorist activity but none of that mattered anymore. Then one day after the murder she was approached by a man who expressed his deepest sympathy at her loss and offered to provide financial help. At that time they had no savings and insufficient income to pay the rent so she gratefully accepted his offer of assistance only to discover later to her amazement that their benefactor was a member of the IRA, one of Pearse Kelly's men.

'I still don't understand why the IRA stepped in to help us but it makes me think that perhaps my father was involved in something to do with them. Either way it makes no difference now, although I'm labelled a Protestant on my birth certificate I couldn't give a toss for either of them. Catholics and Protestants - we're all Irish so why can't we just put the past behind us and get on with living together on this wee island. Sorry for the rant Patrick but I believe that the sooner Ireland is united the sooner we'll get on the road to peace. It may be a long way off but at least an end would be in sight if Ireland is reunited. Things will only get worse in the North as long as we're divided. No surrender and all that crap.' Her rant over Anne grinned at Patrick and said, *'How about a tot of whiskey to help you sleep?'*

'That would be grand.' Replied Patrick as he watched Anne get the bottle of Bushmills Whiskey from the cabinet and pour two large glasses. She was very beautiful and spirited and even the way she poured the whiskey impressed him. Pretending to be her fiancée would not be difficult.

'Here's to the operation, whatever it is.' She said as they clinked glasses and downed the whiskey, *'Now it's my bedtime. I'm afraid that even though to the rest of the world you're my fiancée, you're spending the night on the settee Patrick. I'll get you some blankets and a pillow - you should be fine.'*

Warmed by the whiskey and tired after the eventful day he felt drowsy and despite the attraction, he was disinclined to 'try his hand' with Anne just now. He had felt the chemistry between them from the moment they'd met on the doorstep and now after their conversation there was an added element of respect. She had a fire in her eye and he knew it wouldn't be difficult pretending to be her fiancée, in fact he was looking forward to it. She returned with the bedding and after leaving it on the settee she gave him a quick peck on the cheek and went upstairs to bed. He snuggled down on the comfy settee and within minutes he was fast asleep.

Back in Pearse Kelly's house on the Falls Road, Pearse, Liam, Mick and Karl had spent the day working on the detailed arrangements for the arms shipment. Under pressure from Admiral Dönitz they had agreed through the German Ambassador in Dublin to a date only two weeks away. Telephone calls had been made to contacts in Greencastle where a fishing boat with an IRA sympathising skipper was lined up to handle the transfer of the arms from the submarine. It was decided that the safest place to store the arms short term was on the fishing boat which could then offload them when the conditions were suitable onto a smaller boat for shipment across Lough Foyle into Northern Ireland. The operation was completely weather dependent and anything other than a calm night would require postponement. The arrangement was that the submarine commander would contact Admiral Dönitz's office with a precise location for the rendezvous which would eventually be transmitted to Karl who would be waiting with the fishing boat and his IRA colleagues in Greencastle. It was furthermore decided that if Patrick was successful in getting a job offer at Harland and Wolff he should give his employers advance warning that he might need a few days leave to attend a funeral in Buncrana where his uncle had been told he'd only days to live. It was a high risk chain of actions and events with lots of links, any one of which could lead to disaster. Appropriately, they code-named the operation 'Athchruthú' which was the Irish word for resupply.

'*Right lads,*' said Pearse after he'd made a telephone call to brief Patrick on the plan, '*Hopefully we'll get the white smoke from Patrick tomorrow sometime and after that we're in business.*'

The next morning after breakfast Patrick joined the throng of workers heading for Harland and Wolff as upwards of ten-thousand workers converged like a tidal wave of humanity on the shipyard for the day shift. Meanwhile the nightshift was clocking off and another ten-thousand workers were beginning to make their way home. Harland and Wolff was by far the biggest employer in Belfast and it represented the ultimate example of religious bigotry in the country because every single employee was a Protestant. Discrimination against the Catholic community in Northern Ireland was rife but nowhere was it practiced more diligently than in Harland and Wolff. Not only would a Catholic have no chance of getting a job in the shipyard but were a Catholic to arrive at the yard seeking a job, such was the simmering hatred between the Loyalists and the Nationalists that it was unlikely he would leave in one piece. Virtually without exception in Northern Ireland, Loyalists were Protestants and Nationalists were Catholics - politics and religion were never more entwined.

The men poured though the entrance to the shipyard in a tidal wave and then split up as they made their way to their various work stations, meanwhile Patrick headed for the main office where a long queue of likeminded hopefuls were seeking employment. Eventually, when he arrived at the head of the queue he was asked first to show his birth certificate and then questioned about his trade. When he said he was a welder who had worked for the Irish Steam Packet Company in Dublin he was directed to another shorter queue of those men who had been selected as potential employees. By the time he reached the head of this slower moving queue it was nearly lunchtime but he felt this heart race as the person who had been ahead of him in the queue left the interview room and he was summoned. Behind a table in the otherwise barren room sat five men who would conduct the interview. The leader sat in the middle and as Patrick entered he stood up, shook his hand and invited him to sit in the cane chair opposite them. He then introduced the interview team one-by-one stressing the trade that was the particular speciality of each of them before pointing out that he was the welding expert. What followed was a thorough grilling during which Patrick had the opportunity to describe in detail the work he'd been doing for the Steam Packet Company and to point out that he'd been part of the specialist team which handled the more difficult jobs in the most inaccessible parts of the ship. This clearly impressed the team. When asked for his references he passed the letter he'd received from his previous employer but it barely received more than a glance. *'It's our policy to verify references so we'll be contacting the Steam Packet Company to check your story but if it holds up we'll be wanting you to start immediately - which probably means the day after tomorrow by the time we've checked out your reference. Thanks for coming in Patrick. We'll phone you once we've been in touch with the Irish Steam Packet Company.'* The leader of the panel stood up, shook Patrick's hand again and the interview was over. It had barely lasted fifteen minutes but it had felt like hours. Patrick left the yard on a high and confident that he'd be offered a job. The impression he'd got was that they badly needed welders of his calibre but until he received their call he couldn't be certain of getting a job.

It was afternoon as he walked back towards Sandy Row and by way of a small and perhaps premature celebration he stopped off at the McHugh's Bar for a pint of Guinness. He wouldn't normally be drinking at this early hour in the day but he reckoned he deserved it and his decision was made easier because it had started to rain just as he was approaching the bar. He knew that Anne and her mother would smell drink on him the minute he walked through the door so the shower of rain couldn't have been better timed. He had a plausible excuse for his imbibing. That evening he made a quick call to Pearse to update him on how his interview went. *'Well done Patrick, that sounds very encouraging. When they call the Steam Packet Company they'll get a glowing report of your work. Assuming you get the job you need to break the news about your aged uncle in Buncrana. If everything goes according to plan you will need three, maybe four days at most off work in order to attend the funeral and help close down his affairs.'*

'I'm worried about this Pearse.' He responded, *'Would it not be better if one of you got the training on their plastic explosive and then passed that on to me? Surely it can't be that difficult? Also, it would be a very simple thing for Harland and Wolff to call the local undertakers in Buncrana and check my story. Covering that would further complicate things. How about asking Karl to press the point with the Germans?'*

'Patrick, you're right. Either Liam or Mick can get the training and then pass on what they've learnt to you. It'll also be good for both of them to become familiar with handling German explosives. I'll get onto Karl now and he can talk to the Germans this evening. We should be able to get back to you tomorrow but I think you can assume you'll not be involved in the arms shipment, after all it's up to us to assess the risk and I can't imagine the German version of gelignite being much different from what we're used to. However, you should stay in the house until this has all been agreed and don't pass on any of this to either Anne or her mother, the less they know about the operation the better for everyone, including them.' Said Pearse before hanging up and returning to the kitchen where Karl and the two IRA men were drinking tea. Pearse explained the plan change to Karl who left the room to call the German embassy

in Dublin and pass on the message that having Patrick involved in the arms shipment was too risky because a request for compassionate leave to attend an uncle's funeral in Buncrana so soon after starting in Harland and Wolff would almost certainly arouse suspicion.

'You happy with this lads?' Pearse enquired after Karl had left the room.

Both men nodded and the Mick said, *'I'd like to call my wife and let her know I'll be away for a while.'*

'No problem, you can use the phone when Karl has finished.' Said Pearse who was feeling good about the way things were coming together. At some point he would have to brief the IRA High Command but he still had doubts about how far they could be trusted so he made the decision to wait until the munitions were safely stashed in his Ballyscullion arsenal before he told them. He knew this would invite their wrath but the High Command could add nothing to the operation so he might as well present it to them as a fait accompli once the arms were safely in his hands. Minutes later Karl popped his head through the kitchen door to report that he'd passed on the message to the German ambassador and he then headed back across the hallway to the toilet while Mick got on the phone to his wife. Seated in the toilet he could hear faintly Mick's conversation on the telephone it seemed to Karl that Mick was being careful not to be overheard. It wasn't that he was deliberately eavesdropping but a tiny alarm bell in his head had started ringing. Why was he talking so quietly and was he actually talking to his wife? Even through the toilet door and in spite of Mick's efforts Karl could detect a hushed urgency in his voice and more worrying, there were details of the plan being relayed over the phone that didn't seem to be consistent with what should have been a very straightforward call to his wife. It dawned on him that Mick might not have realised he was in the toilet so he finished up and noisily flushed the toilet. Mick hastily put the receiver down as he emerged from the toilet, *'Things OK with the wife Mick?'* he said with a smile.

'She wasn't exactly over the moon Karl but she knows I'm working on something important. I'll make it up to her when I get back to Dublin.' He replied as a tiny worm turned in his head - how much of his telephone call had Karl been able to hear?

The rest of the day was spent working on the details and phoning contacts in Greencastle. The arms transfer from the submarine to the trawler would be tricky in a number of respects and it was particularly dependent on the weather. In calm conditions it would be possible for the trawler to lie alongside the submarine but in even the slightest swell the transfer would have to be made by shuttling back and forth between the two vessels with a rowing boat. They calculated that to transfer the full shipment would require up to a dozen trips in the rowing boat and that would take a couple of hours at least. Furthermore, the operation would have to be carried out in darkness to avoid being seen from the shore but fortunately that area of Donegal was very thinly populated. A submarine would be hard to see at night and whatever lights were observed from the shore would be assumed to come from fishing boats. However, in even moderately bad weather the operation would have to be postponed or cancelled as it would be much too dangerous. The IRA contact in Greencastle reckoned the chances were less than fifty-fifty and he recommended the transfer was made either in Lough Swilly or Sheephaven, two large inlets on the north coast of Donegal. But that was out of the question to the Germans. Although both loughs were sheltered enough to more or less guarantee flat water, they were too shallow for the submarine to escape underwater should a British warship appear on the scene. The Germans were categorically unprepared to put one of their U-boats at risk on this operation, at a time when the battle of the Atlantic hung in the balance.

They worked on with only a short break for supper and eventually Pearse pronounced that it was time to call it a day and get to bed. *'That's enough for now lads. Tomorrow we should get the news from Patrick that he's secured the job at Harland and Wolff and after that we're in business. I've got a good feeling about this operation and all the pieces seem to be falling into place nicely. See you in the morning.'*

As the team dispersed and headed upstairs to bed Karl hung back and said to Pearse, who was tidying up the papers on the table, *'I need to talk to you urgently Pearse - but not now - could I see you down here a bit earlier than usual for breakfast, say at 7am?'*

'Why can't we talk now Karl,' queried Pearse, alarmed at the worried look on Karl's face.

'Please trust me. You will understand when I tell you.' Said Karl as he left the room and headed upstairs to bed leaving Pearse scratching his head in puzzlement. Something was badly wrong but what could it be? He didn't sleep much that night and the next morning he headed down to the kitchen early to find the German already sitting at the table with a pot of tea and two mugs in front of him. As he was pouring the tea Pearse said, *'Right Karl, what is it? You cost me a night's sleep worrying that something was wrong.'*

'I didn't sleep much either.' Replied Karl who then went on to relate what he'd overheard the previous evening when he'd been in the toilet. He finished off with a half-baked apology for perhaps over-reacting to a perfectly innocent situation, *'Honestly Pearse, I sincerely hope there's nothing to worry about but I couldn't ignore it. I've no wish to cast suspicion at anyone or to disrupt the harmony of this team at this critical stage but I didn't feel I had a choice.'*

For a few timeless minutes Pearse looked intently at the German while his brain tried to process what he'd just heard. Essentially Karl was accusing Mick, a fellow IRA patriot, of being a traitor to the cause and who was now relaying details of operation Athchruthú to either the Irish Intelligence or the British secret services. It was unthinkable, yet how could he ignore what Karl had just told him? It was ironic that immediately prior to Karl asking him to meet before breakfast, he had just finished saying how he had a good feeling about the operation. That had now been shattered and as his mind raced he knew there was no way back. He had just opened his mouth to speak when the kitchen door opened and in walked Mick. *'Morning,'* he said grumpily as he went to the cabinet to fetch another mug, *'I hope you slept better than I did.'*

'Must have been something in that stew we had for dinner last night,' replied Pearse, *'both Karl and I have also had a rough night.'*

Throughout their customary Ulster fry breakfast Pearse wrestled with his dilemma. If he ignored what Karl had told him then there was significant risk that the operation could be compromised. That would be a disaster. Yet if he was act on the information and confront Mick it was highly unlikely that their relationship would ever be the same again, whether he was a traitor or not. Should he trust the German and pursue the issue with Mick or should he dismiss it out of hand? Of course Mick would deny doing anything wrong and he would inevitably accuse him of believing a German rather than a long-term brother-in-arms. Of course the operation's success was more important to him than any friendship but it still stood for something. If he chose to disregard Karl's story, how could he continue with the constant worry that perhaps their plans were being shared with the intelligence services? As for the German, his only motivation was to make operation Athchruthú a total success so he would have had no ulterior motive in raising his concerns about what he'd overheard. Pearse knew he couldn't let this problem fester and that somehow he'd have to decide what to do in the next hour or two. As he worked his way through his breakfast he decided the top priority was to discuss it at length with Liam in private. Meanwhile Mick appeared relaxed as ever, engaging in friendly banter with Karl. Superficially all was well but the the feeling that there might be a traitor in their midst was almost palpable.

Shortly after breakfast his opportunity arose when he and Liam were left alone in the kitchen to do the washing up. As they both stood at the sink Pearse relayed Karl's story to Liam who listened in stunned silence. *'What do you think, Liam?'* he asked when he'd finished.

'Jazus Pearse. This is serious,' said Liam, *'Mick would explode if you confronted him and obviously he would deny it but what then? Is there a chance it is all a big misunderstanding? But if you do confront Mick, innocent of guilty it will seriously damage this team, I can't see Mick being able to work with Karl again and we need Karl on the team so Mick would have to go. I daresay that back in Dublin he would make sure that the High Command got involved and the issue would then quickly escalate out of control and it could easily spell the end of the operation. This is your call Pearse and I don't envy you.'*

'Thanks Liam,' responded Pearse as he slowly worked his way through the remaining breakfast dishes, *'I think we have to take Karl's story seriously and think of a way to test Mick's loyalty without him realising that he's under suspicion. It's too big a risk to ignore. Do you think we could secretly postpone the operation by a week or two but not tell Mick? Then if a bunch of agents turned up in Greencastle and started searching the fishing boats, we'd know for sure he was guilty. If*

they didn't then we'd have to figure out a way of explaining to Mick why we didn't tell him about the postponement and that might be tricky. The way round that would be to arrange for him to be recalled to Dublin just before we postpone the operation but to set that up would mean I'd have to get the High Command involved.'

The two men finished the washing up and made another pot of tea at which point Mick and Karl returned to the kitchen and the conversation reverted to more detailed discussion about operation Athchruthú. As far as Pearse could determine both Karl and Mick were behaving completely normally but the issue of trust was stifling and he soon pleaded the need for some fresh air. *'I'm off for a walk down to the shops. I'll pick up a paper and some more milk. You guys carry on working on who does what and the timing. We should hear soon whether or not Patrick has got the job.'* With that he put on his dog collar and headed out of the door. By the time he returned, an hour later, he had decided on a course of action. He'd remembered Machiavelli's famous dictum *'Keep your friends close and your enemies closer'* and this had led him to the decision to keep Mick on the team but watch him closely at all times. Confronting him with Karl's allegation would achieve nothing other than a furious denial and engineering his return to Dublin would mean involving the IRA High Command in the operation before the arms shipment had been made. That would open up an unwelcome debate about where the arms should be stored and above all else he was determined to keep them under his control in Northern Ireland. With an abundant supply of arms and explosives he could expand his operation and without them his organisation would continue to be little more than an irritant to the forces of law and order in the North. In his earlier discussion with Liam he'd floated the idea of setting a trap for Mick by postponing the shipment and this now became his strategy. Mick would continue to be treated as a trusted member of the team but from the minute the postponement had become the new plan he and Liam would monitor his movements and telephone calls closely to prevent him passing on the revised schedule to the Irish Intelligence Service. The simpler alternative was to prohibit all outgoing telephone calls but that would immediately make him suspect that he'd been rumbled. He called them together in the kitchen and said, *'lads, I think* our schedule for the arms shipment is too tight, also I've checked the calendar and our current schedule coincides with a three-quarter moon which might make things easier for us but against that it makes us much easier to spot from the shore. If we delay by two weeks there will be no moon so that's what we're going to do. Karl, you need to get on the blower to your boss and tell him to rearrange the U-boat drop off. I daresay you'll get a push-back but we call the shots on this so it's not up for debate. I will handle communications with Greencastle and nobody else needs to know about this change to the schedule.' He spoke with an authority that nobody in the room felt like challenging so as he looked at his three companions one after another they nodded. The meeting over, Karl left the room to talk to the Ambassador. He returned a few minutes later and gave them a thumbs-up and said buoyantly, 'I think the ambassador was relieved to hear about the reschedule. It was very tight and I understand that Dönitz was reluctant about redeploying one of his U-boats from a planned attack on a large Atlantic convoy around that time.'

'Good,' responded Pearse, relieved to be back in control of what had the makings of a very troublesome issue. Later that morning while they were waiting for news from Patrick about his job at Harland and Wolff he had a side word with Liam, 'You and I must not let Mick out of our sight from now on and there will be no outgoing telephone calls without my express permission. I didn't say this at our meeting because it would almost certainly have set alarm bells ringing in his head and anyway, it's been an unofficial rule we've all followed up to now.'

After lunch Patrick phoned to confirm that he had got a job as a welder in one of the elite teams which was entrusted with the more technically demanding tasks in the more inaccessible parts of the ship. This was extremely good news because it meant he should be able to hide plastic explosive in places where it would be unlikely to be discovered. When queried about the schedule Pearse was deliberately vague telling him that he'd be informed as soon as it firmed up. He was equally vague about where the arms transfer would take place pointing out that Patrick no longer needed to know anything about that as he was no longer involved in the operation. At some point a meeting would be arranged with him to hand over the plastic explosive and after that it would be up to him to plant it. In the meantime he was instructed to work hard and gain as much acceptance by the welding team as possible while at the same time developing his plan to maximise the damage and delay to the corvette production line which was ramping production up to two new ships a week. He was advised to adopt the mindset of a loyal Harland and Wolff employee who was working in the shipyard for the long haul. Patrick sensed a degree of uncertainty in Pearse's normally decisive tone but he chose not to say anything. He had the feeling the schedule was slipping and although that gave him more time to prepare the ground he was also anxious to get the job done and return to his life Dublin. On the upside it gave him more time with Anne and he wasn't going to complain about that. Even in those first few days he had come to enjoy her company and especially her feisty spirit. Pretending to be her fiancée was fun and the chemistry between them was natural and easy for all to see.

One morning when Anne and her mother were alone together, her mother noted wryly, *'You and Patrick seem to be getting on rather well.'*

'Early days Mum,' she replied, *'I'm just doing my job. We're going out to McHugh's bar this evening, it's really important we're seen to be a couple.'*

That evening they walked hand-in-hand down to the bar. It was a warm summer's evening and a faint breeze from the North was bringing smells of the sea. In a flashback to his youth he remembered his early teens when he was learning to sail in a small dinghy on Loch Swilly. He could still feel the tug of the tiller as he hardened in the simple lug sail so the boat came on the wind and lent over, forcing him to sit out on the weather gunwale. He had never known such freedom. The wind was absolutely free, like horizontal gravity and to harness the power of the wind in the boat seemed as magical as freewheeling down a hill on his bike. His father was proudly watching him from the slipway at Buncrana and he was still there beaming with pride when an hour later Patrick brought the dinghy safely back alongside. They hugged tightly and it was the closest he had ever been to his father. He felt a pang of guilt as he realised it had been months since he last contacted his parents and he resolved to give them a call soon and update them on his latest movements. It might even be possible to visit them he thought, before quickly recognised that this was out of the question while he was engaged on this operation in Harland and Wolff.

As they arrived at the bar he gave her hand a quick squeeze and said, *'OK Anne, let's be an engaged couple for the next couple of hours.'* She kissed his cheek lightly as they entered the busy, smoke-filled bar. Perhaps it was his imagination but no sooner had they stepped inside than he sensed a slight lull in the hubbub as many curious faces turned towards them. Apprehensively he followed her to a large table where she'd spotted several of her neighbours. The introductions over he was quickly put at his ease when one of the men addressed him with false reverence, *'It's the lucky man himself! Well Patrick I wish you all the best. You've got a very special girl there and I hope for your sake you're up to the job. Anne's got spirit - right lads?'* At which the men banged the table and their wives and sweethearts frowned in friendly rebuke. *'Is there something I ought to know?'* Queried Patrick looking intently at Anne. *'You'll find out in time Patrick, in the meantime a woman could die of thirst here unless she gets a drink soon.'*

Four or five pints of Guinness later, he couldn't remember exactly, they excused themselves and said good night to their friends. It had been an evening of pleasant banter, mostly at Patrick's expense but he enjoyed the warmth of their humour. For the first time he felt a pang of guilt about the operation he was embarking on. In a few weeks time he was planning to sabotage the company upon which they all depended for their livelihood. Now that there were faces on the people he would be hurting he began to to have doubts. At the very least he vowed to himself that under no circumstances would he detonate the explosives if there was any chance that one of his new-found friends would be injured. For obvious reasons he decided to keep this to himself as his superiors in the IRA would consider the collateral deaths of a few Protestants as barely worth a second thought. When they arrived back at the house he thanked Anne for the evening and for sharing her friends. He resisted the urge to make pass at her and as before she gave him an affectionate peck on the cheek and disappeared upstairs to bed while he crashed out on the couch. The following day he would start work as a welder in Harland and Wolff.

Back at Pearse's house the rescheduled arms shipment was falling into place. Karl had received confirmation from Dublin that a submarine carrying the munitions was planning to surface off Culdaff on the agreed night. Liam had made contact with the IRA sympathiser who owned one of the fishing boats in Greencastle and without revealing anymore than was absolutely necessary he had received his full support for the plan. Pearse had also made arrangements for the arms to be moved across Loch Foyle and then transported from the shore to the arms stash near Ballyscullion. All that remained for them was to travel to Greencastle on the day before the transfer and rather than risk the heavily patrolled border crossing at Londonderry with a German in the car they would take the long way round and cross the border to Monaghan. After that they'd have a five hour drive around to Greencastle via Sligo on the west coast of Ireland, but this leg of the journey would be in the Irish Free State and so would be relatively stress-free. At one point Mick had casually asked if he could phone his wife but Pearse had refused permission on the grounds that his wife had no need to know about the reschedule. *'But all I want to do is to tell her I'll be back a couple of weeks later than I'd told her last time we spoke,'* he protested.

'No.' Replied Pearse in a tone which made it obvious that it would not be in Mick's best interest to pursue the issue. Later on Mick said he fancied a breath of fresh air and headed for the door. Pearse glanced across at Liam who got the message and said, *'Good idea Mick. I'll come with you.'*

'Grand.' Replied Mick with no detectable hint of either reluctance or enthusiasm. It was only a question of time before Mick realised he was under suspicion but for the moment he seemed at ease. While the two men went for their walk Pearse and Karl went over what Karl had overheard on Mick's telephone call to his wife once again and although no further material evidence of duplicity surfaced Pearse was struck by Karl's openness and his complete lack of any apparent motive for being anything other than totally honest. He had absolutely no axe to grind and although Mick had initially been abusive to him, he didn't appear to bear him any grudge. It seemed to Pearse that Karl had only the best interests of the operation at heart and anyway, what possible motive could he have had for framing Mick? Having embarked on this strategy

it meant secretly monitoring Mick for the next two weeks until the original date for the arms shipment came around and as Pearse mulled over the situation he realised there was another possibility - if he was an agent of the Irish Intelligence Service Mick might 'do a runner' and disappear. This would force another reschedule which would clearly undermine German confidence in the IRA's ability to carry out an operation of this magnitude. If Mick was a double agent it was highly probable that the British would be tipped off about operation and although they would want to intercept the arms shipment the bigger prize was the German U-boat. Once the British got wind that an enemy submarine was in the vicinity of Culdaff they could arrange an ambush which was almost certain to succeed. The arms shipment was a side show. Whether or not Mick might reveal the Harland and Wolff plan was of little consequence because they would have to assume that he had, after which they'd have to get Patrick out of Northern Ireland as soon as possible. Pearse looked across at Karl and for the nth time thought that it was a very complicated war - more a war within a war. The Irish Government was paranoid about being invaded by either the British or the Germans and trying to keep both sides sweet was critical to their recently gained independence. Although he'd inherited a hatred of the British and had it fed to him from his mother's milk until this day the thought of being under the control of the Germans made him shudder. There were stories of German brutality coming from the occupied countries. Was the Athchruthú operation making an invasion by one side or the other more likely? Would it be better for him to help the Irish Government to remain neutral during the conflict and then pick up the quest for Irish reunification once the dust had settled? Big questions which he kept to himself for now. This operation was fully underway and although it could still be aborted by either the IRA or the Germans to do so would have drastic consequences for both him personally and the IRA. Keeping the operation secret from the IRA High Command until the arms shipment was safely stashed at Ballyscullion was a very risky strategy but desperate times called for desperate measures and provided the operation went to plan, he'd be a living legend in the IRA. With these arms the centre of gravity of the organisation would shift to

Belfast where he felt it always should have been following the partition of Ireland.

By coincidence many of the same thoughts were going through Patrick's head at precisely the same time. He had already made some workmate friends in Harland and Wolff so there was a very real prospect of killing one of them when the bomb was detonated. That made it personal, something he'd never had to consider before when he was getting fired up about 'the cause'. What he was doing was very different from the typical IRA bombing operation where there were often many casualties but they were faceless victims. The longer he worked in Harland and Wolff the more friends he would make and the personal it would become. Somehow he had to ensure that whenever the bomb went off there was nobody in the vicinity but if that wasn't possible what would he do? Then there was the question of his deepening relationship with Anne. She had no idea what was being planned and most of her friends were Harland and Wolff employees. What would she think of him if he was responsible for killing any of them?

One evening after her mother had gone to bed he and Anne were having a quiet nightcap in front of the fire. As they sipped their Bushmills whiskey their typically Irish conversation covered everything from religion to the meaning of life. There was a natural pause while both of them stared into the glowing embers and then Anne posed the question, *'Are you going to give me any clue about what you're up to Patrick?'*

'I'd love to share it with you Anne but you know as well as I do that the more people who know about the operation the greater the risk that it will be discovered so it's best you know nothing. It's not that I don't trust you - I do - but it's more a question of your own safety. If it all goes wrong and god forbid I'm exposed, then for sure the authorities would come straight here and you'd almost certainly end up being interned,' he paused and looked directly into her eyes before continuing, *'I'd hate for anything to happen to you or your mother, Anne.'*

'And what would happen to you if you were discovered to be working for the IRA?' She asked with obvious concern.

'I'd be executed - no question.' He replied, raising his eyebrows in mock dismay.

'And if you pull it off - whatever you're doing - what will you do afterwards.'

'The plan is I return to Dublin and take up were I left off working for the Irish Steam Packet Company. However I could well be a wanted man after this operation and if that's the case, I'd be persona non grata in Ireland. The Irish Government can't afford to be seen to be harbouring an IRA fugitive. The British would lean on De Valera and given the precarious situation Ireland Is in he'd happily turn me over to the Brits to preserve Irish neutrality. In that case the only option would be to emigrate - which might not be a bad idea anyway. By the time this is over I'll probably have had enough of fighting for the cause.' He said ruefully. Although the operation had barely just got off the ground, he had already begun to think about the longer term and the prospects didn't look good. Initially he thought he'd be a hero but while that might still be the case, the likelihood was the he'd be a hero without a home.

'Where would you emigrate to?' She queried.

'Probably the United States where there are lots of staunch IRA supporters, the descendants of the millions of Irishmen and women who fled the Great Hunger.' He replied. *'I hear Boston is a good place for IRA men who no longer feel safe in Ireland.'*

'Would you take me with you Patrick McGonigle? After all, I am your fiancée.' She asked coyly.

Slightly taken aback he looked at her for a few seconds as a broad smile spread across his face, *'I suppose I'd have to.'* He said with a chuckle.

In the days that followed he made more friends at work and he quickly earned their respect for his welding skills. He was in a team of elite welders who spent most of their time implementing last minute engineering changes deep in the bowels of the ship. It was highly skilled work with next to no supervision, ideal for his primary purpose of sabotaging the shipyard. Along with ninety percent of the workforce he was assigned to the the Flower Class corvettes where production was being ramped up to two boats a week. He learned rapidly and was soon familiar with the corvette layout and more important its strengths and weaknesses and an embryonic plan started to take shape in his head by the end of his second week. He would sabotage the next corvette to be launched, hopefully causing extensive damage to that ship but also impacting the production line.

In the overall operation the next major event was the arms shipment and shortly afterwards he should get the German plastic explosives and whatever training was required. Then he'd have to figure out how to smuggle it into the shipyard - but that was for later, now he needed to decide where to place the explosives in order to maximise the disruption without endangering any of his colleagues. Most evenings he spent with Anne in McHugh's bar and the more time they spent together the closer they became until one night instead of the usual peck on the cheek he received what could only be described as a passionate kiss. It completely wrong-footed him and by the time he'd recovered his composure she had broken off and was heading upstairs to her room, *'Anne...'* he called softly after her but before he could say anything more she'd thrown a parting smile at him and closed the lounge door behind her. He was left staring at the door as his heart thumped and he wrestled to bring his swirling emotions under control. Was her kiss an invitation to follow her upstairs? But surely if she'd wanted that she would have left the door open when she left the lounge? *'Don't rush into things Patrick.'* He murmured to himself as he arranged the blankets on the sofa and plumped up his pillow, *'you don't want to screw things up.'*

For a long time he lay awake in the darkness watching the flickering light from the fire's dying embers on the ceiling and unable to sleep as a tidal wave of emotion overwhelmed him. He knew he was falling in love and as he tumbled through space towards the unknown, for the first time in weeks his mind was distracted from operation Athchruthú. Their situation was complicated. Living with Anne and her mother meant being careful and guarded. This was a Protestant family with deeply ingrained Protestant values and were he to be discovered in Anne's bedroom by her mother the consequences could be drastic. She could quite easily react by throwing him and possibly her out of the house. Unlikely though that seemed he wasn't prepared to take the risk so he began to plot a trip to the coast which would give them private time together. In order not to arouse suspicion he decided that a suitable cause for celebration would be his first pay packet from Harland and Wolff which was due at the end of the week. He could see about either borrowing a car or catching the bus and then the two of them could take off to the North Coast and stop overnight somewhere. Her mother would probably gently disapprove but he could explain that it would be consistent with the charade they were all involved in. As his heartbeat gradually returned to normal he finally drifted off to sleep, happy to have a plan.

Meanwhile at Pearse's house the atmosphere crackled with suspicion. After a couple of days Pearse was pretty sure that Mick must have realised that he was under constant surveillance however nothing in his behaviour had given that away. It seemed that was unaware of the suspicion he was under, which only served to increase Pearse's conviction that he was an undercover agent for Irish Intelligence. Surely Mick must be aware that he was being watched and if he was innocent wouldn't he be asking what was going on? The original date for the postponed arms shipment was fast approaching so if Mick was an agent he now had only had a few days to alert his contacts of the changed schedule. If the Irish authorities turned up in Greencastle and started searching the fishing boats then it was certain Mick was a traitor. Since the arms shipment had been delayed Mick had been barred from using the phone. He'd also been accompanied on every outdoor excursion by either him or Liam and so now if he did want to inform his handler of the change he was running out of time.

One morning after breakfast Mick announced that he was going for a walk and as usual Liam invited himself to accompany him as he also claimed he needed some fresh air. *'Grand,'* said Mick, *'Let's be off then.'*

They walked slowly along The Falls Road past the Royal Victoria Hospital when suddenly, as they were passing a red post box, Mick reached into his inside pocket for a letter which he was on the brink of posting when Liam realised what was happening. *'Stop! What are you doing, Mick?'* He cried out, quickly placing himself between Mick and the letterbox.

'Christ Liam - what's the matter with you? I'm just wanting to post a letter to the wife. Is there anything wrong with that?' He enquired, obviously hurt by the inference that he couldn't be trusted.

Wrong-footed, for a moment Liam had no idea how to react. Mick was his friend, they'd gone to school together and been brothers in arms in the IRA for years yet there were reasonable grounds to suspect he was an agent for Irish Intelligence and this recent attempt to post a letter seemed to add to the case against him. 'I'm sorry Mick but I need to see the letter - please give it to me.' He said looking directly into his friend's eyes. There was a moment's hesitation and then Mick handed Liam the letter saying, 'There you are - see - it's a letter to my wife, like I told you.'

Liam stared hard at the envelope which was clearly addressed to Mrs M O'Reilly. What now? He glanced back up at his friend and was on the brink of apologising when he felt there was something strange about the envelope which seemed to be much thicker than he expected. Wanting to believe that Mick was innocent of any disloyalty to the IRA but still with Karl's relaying of the overheard telephone call in his mind he half apologised, 'Mick, we're all really edgy and maybe I've over-reacted but with so much riding on this operation we mustn't risk any leaks however unintentional. If you want to post a letter to your wife then it will be up to Pearse to decide.' He then pointedly put the envelope in the inside pocket of his jacket, now almost certain that the letter contained more than just a sheet or two of writing paper. 'Let's go back to the house and we can settle this with Pearse.' Mick looked at him with a mixture of hurt and indecision in his eyes. For a few seconds Liam thought that he might flee but eventually he simply nodded and turned to walk back up the Falls Road towards the house. Not a word passed between them until they entered the kitchen where Pearse and Karl were chatting over mugs of tea. Pearse looked up as they came in and immediately knew something was wrong. Liam glanced at him and then looked across at Karl, 'Karl, would you mind leaving us for a while? - I'll call you when were'd done.'

'Certainly.' He replied, immediately getting to his feet and leaving the room. He had a feeling he knew what was coming but he also knew when he wasn't wanted. The relationship between him and Pearse was never going to be anything but businesslike but he felt that he'd earned his trust. In any event the operation couldn't go ahead without him so he had no reason to feel insecure. He was confident that whatever the three IRA men wanted to discuss in private, it wasn't about him.

The atmosphere in the kitchen was very tense. Pearse listened intently as Liam recounted how he'd intercepted Mick's attempt to post a letter to his wife which was a clear contravention of their self-imposed communications blackout.

'So what's your explanation Mick?' Enquired Pearse.

Mick cleared his throat before responding, *'I know I shouldn't have Pearse, but me and the wife have been going through a bad patch recently and her not knowing where I am and having no idea when I'll be back, or even if I will be back has made things ten times worse. I'm scared she's going to leave me. For a while I thought I might have to step down from operational duties until things settled down a bit between us. I just wanted to tell her that I'd be back a bit later than I'd previously told her over the phone.'* He glanced nervously between his two comrades, looking for signs of sympathy and support, but finding none he coughed self-consciously and continued, *'If you give me the letter back I'll burn it in the Rayburn before your eyes and then can we get back to normal?'* and he reached behind his chair to open the door in the cooker revealing the glowing embers of the fire.

Pearse looked at him intently and then at Liam, *'Sounds fair to me Liam?'* He replied, *'What do you think?'*

With the ball now clearly in his court he reached into his inside pocket and withdrew the letter before speaking carefully, *'Mick, we go back a long way and we're not just brothers in arms, we're also mates. I'm sorry to hear that you and the Missus are going through a sticky patch and I hope it all sorts itself out soon. Maybe I am a bit edgy but when I saw you starting to post this letter I had to stop you and I hope you'd have done the same if you'd been in my position.'* He was in the process of handing the letter to Mick when Pearse intervened.

'Mind if I see that Liam?' For a moment he hesitated. Mick's hand was already outstretched but before he could take the letter Pearse quickly grabbed it. Liam was watching Mick and the fear in his eyes was unmistakable. For a few seconds Pearse fingered the letter carefully

while looking at the address. He was obviously wondering what to do next as Mick shifted his extended hand across towards Pearse. Thinking that he was on the point of snatching the letter Liam blurted out, *'Pearse, there's something fishy about the letter - it seems far too thick as if it contains something other than a sheet of writing paper, don't you think?'*

Pearse looked up from the letter and stared directly at Mick and then down at his outstretched hand which remained where it was, only inches from the letter. *'Not so fast Mick, I'm afraid we're going to have to take a look inside before we burn it. That'll be OK with you?'* He said as he carefully opened the envelope. *'What have we here?'* He added as he opened the envelope and withdrew its contents revealing not just a sheet of paper but also another envelope. *'I see this is addressed to a gentleman at the McKee Barracks Mick. Care to explain?'* He said as he ripped open the second envelope and glanced quickly at the contents. It was as he expected, a brief note to Military Intelligence informing them that the project had been delayed by two weeks.

Within the ranks of the IRA there was none more despised than the traitor. Loyalty to the cause was the bond which held them together and whenever a double agent was discovered in the ranks, it inevitably spelt death and usually after a lengthy period of harsh interrogation in order to establish what secrets had been revealed and over what period of time. All three men were fully aware of what lay in store for Mick and there was little he could say in his defence however, with anguish and fear showing in his eyes, he said, *'Pearse, about three months ago I was anonymously grassed to the Intelligence as a member of the IRA. One night they came to the house and told me and my wife that we'd both be interned immediately and then tried for terrorism unless I worked for them. They said they had enough information on me to see that I hanged and my wife would get a long prison sentence. I had no choice so I agreed to work for them.'* He breathed deeply in a vain attempt regain his composure but his lip was still quivering when he continued, *'I swear I've only told them the absolute minimum and I've never revealed any names. They threatened me with interrogation but I told them I'd sooner die than grass on my friends. They backed off but not before threatening to pursue the issue further if they were unhappy with the information I was giving them. I've mentioned no names on this operation and all they've been interested in is the arms shipment. They know nothing about the plan to sabotage the Harland and Wolff shipyard.'* His appeal fell on deaf ears as Pearse mockingly replied, *'Dress it up how you like Mick but the bottom line is you're a traitor and you will be executed. The only question is when - and you could possibly delay your E-day by becoming a double agent. Feeding Military Intelligence misleading and false information could keep them off our backs for a while but for that to work we'd have to trust you. Can you think of any reason we should trust you Mick?'*

Mick squirmed in his seat looking backwards and forwards between Pearse and Liam before visibly slumping. *'That's for you to decide. I don't want to waste your time trying to persuade you that I deserve your trust. But my contact is expecting an update from me - in fact it's overdue - so I could feed him whatever message you wanted?'*

'And when your contact realises you gave them duff information, don't you think they will smell a rat? They'd almost certainly conclude that you'd become a double agent.' Said Pearse. *'Liam and I will talk it over and you're going upstairs to be handcuffed to the bed.'* He nodded towards Liam who then led Mick out of the room. He returned a couple of minutes later to be greeted by Pearse. *'You did well Liam - and now I think we should update Karl. It's weird but I trust the German more than I trust Mick. We'll leave him to sweat for a bit and you and I will decide what to do later. There's no hurry.'*

Karl felt vindicated that his alertness had led to the exposure of Mick as traitor and he felt more a part of the team than ever. Later that day he confirmed the new schedule with the Embassy and that was followed with several hours on the telephone to Greencastle setting up the rendezvous with the U-boat. As before, their major worry was bad weather and how to cope with a postponement. Two plans were developed. One was to reschedule the shipment by up to twenty-four hours and if the bad weather looked like continuing the transfer would be switched to Lough Swilly which was more sheltered but was also a potential trap for the U-boat should the British navy turn up unexpectedly. Pearse was understandably reluctant to default to the Loch Swilly handover because it meant that the arms would be arriving outside his sphere of control and the last thing he wanted was the High Command involved in the arms shipment. The current plan ensured that the munitions would never actually be landed in Donegal and would remain on the trawler until they were transhipped across Lough Foyle into Northern Ireland. Then and only then Pearse intended to disclose full details of the operation to the IRA High Command in Dublin. Karl expressed his deep concern that Mick may already have compromised the sabotage operation but after some discussion they decided that if that had been the case, surely they would have arrested Pat as soon as they knew he was a member of the IRA? There was undoubtedly an increased risk to the sabotage operation but they decided that while there was no indication that the plan had been uncovered they would press ahead. They also decided it was best that Pat knew nothing about Mick's exposure as an agent of the Irish Military Intelligence. He had enough on his plate as it was.

Afterwards Pearse went to talk to Mick on his own, *'Mick, you've said that your handler has no knowledge of the sabotage operation in Harland and Wolff. You know the deal with the Germans was half the shipment up front and the other half after the operation was complete. Have you told them this?'* He questioned softly as Mick visibly cowered beside the bed, his wrist held high by the handcuff which was attached to the metal frame at the head of the bed. The fear in his eyes had no effect on Pearse who had been there before. This wasn't the first time he'd had to interrogate and execute a traitor and he knew Mick knew that. *'You might as well tell me the truth, Mick.'* He said as he waited patiently for his response.

'Pearse, they know there are two shipments but as I've said already they are only interested in intercepting the arms. That's all they cared about so they know nothing about the sabotage plan.' He replied with a loud sigh of resignation, he knew he was going to die and it was only a question of when and how painfully. Bodies of executed traitors usually bore witness to the brutality of their killing. No attempt was ever made to conceal from the members of the IRA the consequences of betraying the cause.

Pearse looked at him intently for a while as he thought about what Mick had told him and then without a word he abruptly turned and left the room. Back in the kitchen Liam was staring into a mug of tea. He looked up immediately with raised eyebrows and said, *'How did that go Pearse?'*

They talked it over for more than an hour before concluding that they had to accept the increased risk and continue with the sabotage plan otherwise the arms shipment would be cancelled. A more dangerous option was briefly considered and almost immediately rejected - *'what if they pulled Pat out of Harland and Wolff and cancelled the sabotage operation entirely but didn't tell the Germans?'* That way they would get the arms shipment but at what price? Making an enemy of the Germans was definitely a bad idea for all sorts of reasons so they decided to keep Pat in the dark. There was little point in adding to his problems when there was nothing he could do about it but they both acknowledged that Pat's position had become more precarious.

Oblivious of all this Pat was focusing on the weekend up north with Anne. He organised a bus trip to Ballycastle on the North Coast which got them there late on Friday evening and returned to Belfast on Sunday morning. This would give them a full day on Saturday to explore the area on bicycles which the Marine Hotel had promised to make available. Pat was determined to make this a special weekend so he'd blown the budget and reserved the best room in the hotel which overlooked the harbour, Rathlin Island and to the east the geometrically perfect profile of Fair Head. As the day approached he could barely contain his excitement. In McHugh's Bar on the Thursday they had told their friends about their trip up North and had to endure some good-natured banter. *'Aren't you supposed to have the honeymoon after the wedding?'* Asked one of the welding team to sniggers from around the table. With no good answer to hand Pat replied in the spirit of the question, *'We like to do things differently - don't we, Anne?'* He responded, realising too late that his comment was open to a more risqué interpretation, *'Oh you do, do you! Any hot tips for us then Pat?'* His pal replied to a round of table-thumping from half the bar who had clearly been listening intendedly. Anne blushed and tried to change the subject but for the remainder of the evening the table rocked with laughter as the art of the double-entendre was taken to extremes that only the Irish could reach. Back at the house he made a brief call to update Pearse on his plan to take Anne away for the weekend and also to tell him that he now had the makings of a plan for the sabotage. He chose not to go into details just yet and before then someone had to get the plastic explosives to him and show him how to handle it. For the moment the ball was firmly in Pearse's court.

The journey North on the bus took nearly three hours with stops at Antrim, Ballymena and Ballymoney before finally arriving at Ballycastle. Although it was the weekend the bus was quiet and they enjoyed sitting together looking out of the window as the bus trundled through the agricultural landscape of Northern Ireland. Anne fell asleep for a while, dropping her head onto his shoulder as she slumbered. He knew vaguely what was happening to him but his swirling emotions had no clear form, this was unknown territory and he knew he had to tread carefully. On arrival they checked in as Mr and Mrs McGonigle and were shown up to their room. Anne gasped with delight, *'What a beautiful room! And the view - I can hardly believe it.'* It was a still evening and the sun had just dipped beneath the northwest rim of the world, painting the high cirrus clouds in streaks of red and gold. Beneath them lay the tiny harbour with the usual collection of small fishing boats and punts and across a glimmering stretch of sea Rathlin Island with its shining white cliffs filled the horizon. She stared in frozen amazement while Pat lifted their suitcase onto the double bed and started unpacking it, *'Have you noticed Fair Head over there to the east? That's where we're going tomorrow.'* He said, feeling more excited than he had ever felt in his life before. Looking over at Anne who was silhouetted against the window, mesmerised by the view he knew this was 'it'. *'I mustn't mess this up!'* he said to himself as he fought to contain the urge to blurt out his love for this incredible woman who had exploded into his life like a bombshell. Anne turned and with undiluted joy written all over her face said, *'This is really perfect Pat. I've not been up north before and I never imagined it could be so beautiful. Thank you for arranging it all, right now I couldn't be happier.'*

In the dining room later they sat at a table for two by the window and as they enjoyed their meal and shared a bottle of wine they watched as the sunset faded into darkness with the stars piercing the night sky like tiny diamonds, twinkling pinpricks of brilliant light. *'Do you realise that the light from those stars could have been travelling through space for a thousand years before arriving here and if one of them exploded and disappeared, its last rays would continue to streak across the cosmos for all those years to shine on us here in Ballycastle and then in an instant it would vanish. Imagine what it would be like to experience that!'*

'You are a true Irishman Patrick McGonigle - a romantic dreamer at heart.' She responded with a broad smile as she reached across the table and took his hand. Her touch was like a kiss and again he felt himself falling into the Infinity of her eyes. He was adrift without a rudder on an ocean of love. *'Patrick, you can let go of my hand now, I'm not going anywhere.'* She said gently so as not to awaken him too abruptly from his reverie. *'You were miles away - I hope in a nice place?'*

'Sorry,' he said, *'You're right, I was miles away. Must be in heaven - I'm having dinner with an angel.'*

She squeezed his hand and flashed a smile, *'As I just said, a true Irishman - full of the blarney! Let's go to bed now, we've a long day ahead and it's years since I last rode a bicycle.'* Keeping hold of his hand she stood up and led him through the dining room door saying goodnight to the head waiter on the way. *'Hope you enjoyed your meal.'* He said with a wink to Pat as he was led out of the restaurant and upstairs to their bedroom. But Pat didn't notice the wink, he only had eyes for Anne. *'Let's not pull the curtains tonight so we can look out at the stars.'* She said as she got ready for bed.

They were awakened as the first ray of sunshine fell across their sleeping faces. Fair Head stood angular and black against the pink dawn sky and a path of rippled gold led to the horizon where the morning sun had just poked its head above the gleaming sea. It was going to be a perfect day. After a leisurely 'Ulster fry' breakfast they collected their packed lunches from the hotel kitchen and set off for the six mile ride to Fair Head. The first stretch was along the relatively busy A2 but after about three miles they picked up the Torr Head Road and followed that until the turnoff for Fair Head. From there until at most a hundred yards from the cliff edge they were on a very rough farm track which was mainly used by tractors and then only infrequently as the farmland on Fair Head was barren and unsuitable for cultivation. They were forced to push their bikes for the last stretch, dumping them where the track finally petered out beside Lough Doo. Tired after their cycle they lay on the grass in the sun for a while and shared a mug of coffee from the flask. The sun shone in a cloudless sky and a faint north westerly breeze gently cooled them as they sipped their coffee.

'Special place, don't you think Anne?' Said Pat, opening his arms wide as if to embrace the view.

'I'm lost for words Pat.' She replied, *'All I can think of to say is - thank you for bringing me here.'*

'We have a choice now.' Said Pat as he unfolded the map on his lap and Anne shuffled along the grass to sit close beside him. *'Look here - at the top of this lough - there's a steep track called The Grey Man's Path which would take us down to the bottom of the cliffs. Or we could go right up to the edge of the cliff and just admire the view? Your choice.'*

'Maybe we could do both? But let's go up to the edge first and then if we've got time we could perhaps go down that path - but it looks a bit steep to me.' She said, grabbing his hand and dragging him to his feet. *'We can have our lunch there and soak up the view and the sun. For some reason Pat, I feel that at the moment 'being' is more important than 'doing' - if you know what I mean.'*

They strolled hand-in-hand the short distance to the tip of the headland where the cliffs fell vertically for about three hundred feet to the scree below. They dropped their small rucksack on a flat boulder which would serve as a table for their lunch and cautiously approached the perfectly chiselled edge of the cliff. It was so sharp they could have sat down and dangled their feet over the precipice. Beneath them stood vast pillars of columnar basalt, crystallised lava from an ancient volcanic eruption which had inundated much of the northwest corner of Ireland in ancient times. The scree which tumbled for a further hundred and fifty feet to the sea was comprised of shed-sized boulders which had fallen from the cliffs above. *'Looking at that,'* said Pat, pointing at the scree beneath them, *'I think we'd find it rather difficult to do anything down there - unless you like scrambling - so my thought is we should stay up here and as you said, soak it all up.'*

For a while there was silence between them as each was lost in their own thoughts and then, pointing to the east Pat said, *'Look over there Anne, that's the Mull of Kintyre and it's only eleven miles away and directly over the top of the Mull do you see those high mountains? That's the island of Arran in the Firth of Clyde. There are fierce tides between here and the Mull and if you look beneath us there - about half way between here and the southern tip of Rathlin - you can just see the starting of one of the fiercest whirlpools in the world, it's called Slough-na-More. Even in calm weather like now it's impressive but can you imagine what it's like in a northwesterly gale when the tide is flowing at 8 knots directly into the wind? No ship could survive that! Did you know that six hundred years ago Robert the Bruce is supposed to have hidden in a cave on Rathlin and according to the legend he watched the spider trying over and over again to establish a web across a crevice in the rock. That's where the expression - if at first you don't succeed, try, try and try again - comes from.'* He paused and looked down at Anne who was smiling at him, *'I hope I'm not boring you?'* He said, *'I just love our country Anne, and I can't stop talking about it.'*

'You're not boring me Pat, far from it. I'm fascinated. Please carry on.' She replied, squeezing his hand tightly.

'Do you know Anne, I feel just as Irish standing here as I do standing on Malin Head - which you can just see beyond that big headland in the far distance. It seems daft that technically this is a different country - the North I mean. Here we're at war with Germany and just over there the rest of Ireland is neutral. In the short time I've been working at Harland and Wolff I've made as good or better friends than I've ever had in the Free State. They're all Protestants and all my other pals are Catholics. What is it about the Irish that religion is so divisive? Is there any real difference between us all, other than the way we were brought up? Why is it that religion so defines us and to a large extent determines our path through life?' He shook his head and once again stretched his arms out wide but this time with his palms held upwards in a gesture of confusion and incredulity as he looked to the sky, *'and why are we prepared to die fighting each other when we're all bloody Irishmen! Let me ask you this Anne, do you feel British or Irish?'*

'I've never really thought about it before but standing here, right now with you, I feel Irish first and British a long way second.' She replied, *'yet if it hadn't have been for the conflict our paths might never have crossed - so I've got the war and partition to thank for meeting you.'*

For a long while they stood on the edge of Fair Head in silence holding hands before Pat continued, *'That headland over there,'* he said, pointing to the west, *'that's the Giant's Causeway where Finn MacCool started chucking stones across at his enemy in Scotland. At least that's how the legend goes but there is an island just across the sea in the Hebrides called Staffa which has the identical columnar basalt construction of the Causeway and Fair Head. And here's something else, did you know that in the autumn of 1588 the remains of the Spanish Armada fought their way back to Spain across this stretch of sea. Rumour has it that one of the galleons perished on this coastline in a huge gale. Imagine how dramatic it would have been to have watched that from here? And imagine how terrifying it must have been for the sailors knowing their ship was doomed?'*

'We might not have been standing so close to the edge then!' She replied, taking a step back. *'You know Pat, I think I suffer slightly from vertigo. When I look down at the sea from here I almost feel as if I am falling.'*

He looked at her again and the vertigo he felt was nothing to do with the cliff. His emotions were spinning like Slough-na-More in a storm, *'Falling? Anne I have already fallen. I've fallen in love with you.'*

To his utter delight there was no shocked surprise in her eyes, only a smile so beautiful he knew he would remember it until the day he died. Time stood still. His senses were so heightened, so tuned into the here and now, that he could feel even the faintest brush of the breeze on his cheek, he could smell the scent of the sea as if he was swimming in it and he could hear every bird song as if it was being performed only for him. When she embraced him the press of her body made him tingle with joy. They broke apart and she said, *'This is the happiest day of my life, Pat. I've been in love with you for ages but I kept it to myself for fear of scaring you off. To hear you say 'I love you' is something I will treasure for the rest of my life - no matter what happens. I only wish we could run away and forget about the IRA, religion, the border, the war* and whatever it is you are planning at Harland and Wolff - but I know we can't. Promise me Pat that when it's all over we'll come back to this part to this special place and make our own plans for the rest of our lives.'

'I promise.' He said looking straight into her eyes, 'I promise.' He repeated earnestly.

They returned to the flat boulder and sat side by side in silence while they ate their sandwiches and drank what was left of the coffee until eventually Pat said, 'I don't want this day to ever end but we will soon have to set off back to Ballycastle. It's over there and if you look carefully you can see the window of our room at the Marine Hotel. Tonight we'll leave the curtains open again and from our bed we'll be able to see this exact spot.'

When they'd finished their lunch and packed up they walked hand-in-hand back to their bikes past the narrow entrance to the Grey Man's Path which led down to cliff bottom. It was steep and unwelcoming so both were quick to agree they'd made the right decision to leave it until another day. They mounted their bikes and being downhill they made short work of the return journey to the hotel. It was late afternoon in Ballycastle when the leant the bikes against the wall of a nearby café and bought two ice cream cones, a rare luxury in the days of rationing both north and south of the border. Sitting on the wall overlooking the harbour they gazed out across the Sound of Rathlin and licked their cones like children.

Less than thirty miles away as the crow flies, at precisely the same time although they were not to know it, an Irish trawler was pulling alongside the pier in the village of Greencastle at the entrance to Lough Foyle. They'd had a successful couple of days off the northeast coast of the Malin peninsula and the boat was laden with fish. When their shore warps were fast, three unfamiliar characters emerged from the Harbour Master's office and stood by the docked trawler. One of them waved at the skipper who was in the deckhouse tidying up the paperwork before they started unloading the boxes of fish. He opened the side window and called out, 'Can I help you? Is there something you want?'

'We're coming on board and we have a warrant to search your boat,' the man on the dock replied.

'You're welcome so long as you don't slow up the unloading - you see that lorry over there? He's heading to Dublin with our catch and we're already a bit late.' Replied the skipper. 'Are you with the fisheries or something?' He said as they climbed on board.

'You could say that.' Their leader said, 'everyone needs to stay on board while we do the search.'

'OK,' said the skipper, 'but I'd like to see the warrant and your identity - if you don't mind?'

The man showed him both and then he and his two colleagues proceeded to look with increasing frustration beneath every floorboard and in every cupboard, nook and cranny on the ship.

'If you told me what you were looking for I might be able to help you.' Said the skipper, 'now can I start unloading the fish?'

The man stared at him fixedly for a few seconds before leaping ashore. He had the feeling the trawler skipper knew something which he wasn't telling him so he shouted one last question, 'did you drop off any of your catch at Culdaff by any chance?'

The skipper could think of several sarcastic replies but instead he bit his tongue, these didn't seem to be the sort of people who would appreciate a smart remark, 'No,' he replied 'and I hope you lads find what you're after.' But by then they were walking away.

Shortly afterwards word reached Pearse that agents from the Irish Military Intelligence had turned up in Greencastle and had searched each of the trawlers as they returned to port after the night's fishing. It was apparent that Karl had indeed overheard Mick passing on the details of the arms shipment, so two things were now clear. First, this was positive confirmation that Mick was a traitor and second, the Irish Military Intelligence obviously didn't know about the reschedule. It should now be safe to go ahead with the arms shipment but doubt lingered on whether Pat had already been exposed or not. Pearse's top priority was to get the munitions and he couldn't relax until that shipment had been successfully stashed in his secret arsenal near Ballyscullion. Only then could he refocus on meeting their part of the bargain, the sabotage of the corvette production line at Harland and Wolff. His immediate priority however was to dispose of the traitor. It was the IRA's practice to dump the bodies of traitors on or near an army barracks or police station, not only to let the authorities know that another mole had been dug up and executed but the IRA knew that there were always reporters hanging around the entrances to these places in the hope of picking up a story. To deter any potential informers, the bodies of the executed men were usually mutilated in the traditional IRA manner - they'd be knee-capped. Knee-capping was a gruesome punishment which invariably left the victim crippled for life. In extreme cases bullets were also fired at close range through wrists and ankles. Pearse found the process rather distasteful but acknowledged that it was necessary. In normal circumstances he would have ordered someone else to carry it out and in every terrorist organisation there were people who relished the task, but in these circumstances it was down to either Liam or himself and it wouldn't look right if he ordered Liam to do it. Liam and Mick were lifetime pals and it would have been unnecessarily cruel to force Liam to execute his friend. Pearse sighed deeply, screwed the silencer onto his forty-five revolver and went to see Mick. Both Liam and Karl knew what was about to take place but neither had the slightest desire to witness it so they remained silent in the kitchen waiting for the inevitable. They didn't have long to wait. shortly after hearing the bedroom door close behind Pearse, they heard the unmistakable sound of a silenced revolver - three pops in reasonably quick succession, one in each knee and then one to the head. *'At least he didn't suffer for long.'* Thought Liam. Later that day they obscured the number plates on the car and pushed his mutilated dead body out of the rear door as they sped past the police barracks at the end of the Falls Road. Pearse was happy to see a couple of the regular reporters race out of the nearby café with their cameras at the ready. *'Vultures.'* He muttered, *'But everyone's gotta live I suppose.'*

Three days before the rescheduled arms shipment was due to be made Pearse, Liam and Karl set off to make their way to Greencastle. Pearse dearly wished they didn't have to be accompanied by the German Military Attaché but despite a lengthy debate on the subject they concluded that not only was he needed to handle translation but in reality they were probably undermanned for the actual transfer between U-boat and the trawler. Dressed as a priest and with Liam carrying an Irish passport, crossing the border into Donegal wouldn't have presented a serious problem for them but with an important German officer in the car, the risks were considerably greater. Consequently they were forced to take the long way round and cross the border to Monaghan and then drive for six hours or more to Greencastle on roads which remained inside the Republic of Ireland the entire way. The shortest route would have been to cross the border in the vicinity of Londonderry and although there were plenty of IRA supporters in the city who would willingly help them, there was also a strong British Army presence and the risk was deemed too great. They'd received the good news that the Irish agents had left Greencastle soon after searching the last of the local trawlers so now everything depended on the weather. That evening after successfully crossing into Southern Ireland they were once again ensconced in the familiar Monaghan safe-house chatting with their hosts as they worked their way through a bottle of Jamieson's Whiskey. The conversation ranged widely with lengthy debates about how long Britain could survive and would Germany occupy Ireland or would the British jump the gun if that looked probable and occupy the country again after only so recently having been driven out. They all agreed Irish neutrality was a precarious balancing act and there were mixed views on the IRA's strategy of working with Germany with the longer term goal of reuniting Ireland once the war was over. The discussion was becoming heated and going nowhere so Pearse adeptly brought it to an end as he looked across at their somewhat mystified German colleague who was privately baffled that IRA members were allowed to openly express such different views on something so important as the overall strategy of the organisation. Sensing Karl's mild discomfort he said with a smile, *'Karl, time for a bit of a geography lesson. Greencastle is in Donegal on the Malin peninsula which has the reputation for being one of the stormiest places around the British Isles. Of course you probably already know that although the Irish Free State is an independent republic, like it or not it's still geographically one of the British Isles. What is generally referred to as Britain is in fact properly called the United Kingdom of Great Britain and Northern Ireland. So Northern Ireland is not actually part of Great Britain - the word Great referring only to the fact that it is the larger of the two islands that together make up the British Isles. Britain comprises England and*

Scotland, and when you add in Wales you get Great Britain - OK so far Karl?' Struggling to keep up, Karl said nothing so Pearse glanced around the table at his smiling colleagues and then continued, *'The northernmost point of Donegal is Malin Head, a very dangerous spot with rocks and fierce tides ripping between the headland and Inishtrahull, a small island which is a mile offshore. Malin Head is actually the most northerly point of Ireland but it lies in Southern Ireland.'* Karl's brow furrowed deeply and he was in the process of deciding how to respond when one of the men sitting around the table could no longer contain himself and burst into laughter, soon to be followed by the rest of his colleagues.

'It seems illogical.' Said Karl hesitatingly when the laughter died down.

'Ah, but not to an Irishman.' Said Liam.

The following evening the two IRA men and the German arrived safely in Greencastle and met up with the skipper of the trawler who welcomed them on board and showed them below, *'This is the best I can offer you in the way of accommodation, I'm afraid.'* He said, *'Make yourselves at home as best you can. If things go according to your plan you'll only have to endure these conditions for two nights.'*

'This'll do fine, Paddy.' Replied Pearse, *'How's the weather looking for tomorrow night?'*

'So far so good Pearse,' he replied, *'but you know it's the BBC's Shipping Forecast that we're relying on…'*

Twenty-four hours later as darkness was falling they were jilling around in a lazy swell a mile off the coast of Donegal just north of the village of Culdaff. The wind was a light westerly and although they could have done without the swell, in all other respects it was the perfect night for the rendezvous with the U-boat. All they could do now was wait and hope that the German submarine turned up as planned. As night fell the cloud cover increased and the offshore breeze freshened a little, carrying the scent of freshly mown grass and the quiet sounds of the land across the water to the trawler. To the north and clearly visible the lighthouse on Inishtrahull swept its ghostly white light across them every twenty seconds and further out to sea in the north Atlantic the lights of a convoy from America was steaming slowly past on its way to

Liverpool. Pearse wondered privately how many ships from that convoy had been sunk by the U-boat they were about to meet. He shuddered to think of how terrible it must be for those merchant seamen who were risking their lives to keep Britain fed. He'd heard that when a ship was torpedoed and went down any survivors were abandoned to their fate. Under orders not to stop the next ship in the line ploughed straight through the wreckage and the drowning men, their desperate cries clearly audible to the crew who knew that they could be next. On arrival at Liverpool they would have a few days of relative peace before going through the whole experience again. At times Pearse wondered if collaborating with the Germans was a good idea in the longer term. Surely it was only a matter of time until the United States of America once again threw its hat in the ring to defend the British and when that happened, although it might take a long time, Germany would eventually be defeated and what then? The IRA enjoyed widespread sympathy in the USA, particularly amongst the descendants of the families that had emigrated from Ireland during and after the Irish famine of 1845 and most of the IRA's financial support came from their donations. Without their funding the organisation would be not much more than a powerless group of Irish nationalist dreamers. If the USA joined the war against Germany and the sons of American IRA sympathisers were called up to fight and die in support of the British, how many of those sympathisers would be happy continuing to make donations to an organisation which was directly assisting the enemy? He sighed and reconciled himself pragmatically to the fact that the only way the IRA could acquire arms at present was from the Germans so even though he wasn't overly comfortable collaborating with the such a brutal fascist regime, for now the end justified the means.

Time dragged by as they waited in the darkness and then suddenly they glimpsed a light blinking the signal that had been agreed. Karl was the first to recognise it, *'Our U-boat has arrived!'* he shouted in a mixture of excitement and relief. He had avoiding thinking what the reaction of his IRA colleagues might have been if the U-boat hadn't turned up. They signalled the response as the trawler skipper fired up the engine and they chugged the mile or so to where the dark and menacing shape of the German submarine lay. When they came close enough Karl called across to the U-boat captain who was standing in the conning tower with several of his men. They exchanged greetings in German and soon boxes of munitions were being carried onto the deck of the submarine. The trawler's tender was quickly launched and soon everyone was engaged in transporting the heavy boxes of munitions. In the lazy swell the submarine was moving up and down and rolling from side to side, making it difficult to transfer the boxes into the tender but two hours later twenty heavy boxes filled with guns, ammunition and explosives had successfully been transferred. When the final box was lifted off the deck of the U-boat the Captain bade Karl farewell with what seemed a strangely out of place *'Heil Hitler'* and within seconds it had submerged, presumably to continue its deadly mission in the North Atlantic.

'So much for the explosives training we're supposed to have needed but anyway, well done lads.' Said Pearse as the trawler started its engine and made to shoot its net. *'Now we need to catch a few boxes of fish to put on top of this lot. I'm not expecting anybody will want to search us when we get back into Greencastle but you never can be sure. Also, it would invite suspicion if we had nothing to unload when we dock.'*

It was a good night for fishing and by dawn they had filled the net and sorted the catch into fish boxes which now completely covered the twenty cases of arms. They docked at the pier in Greencastle and unloaded the catch to the waiting truck which immediately sped off down the road towards Londonderry. Pearse and Liam remained below for a couple of hours working on the next phase of the plan to get the arms safely across the lough and carried to the secret arms cache near Ballyscullion. Karl wasn't invited to participate so he whiled away the time on the bridge admiring the view. It was a beautiful day and after the intense overnight activity he was content to relax and soak up the stunning scenery. He marvelled at how peaceful everything was and how small and irrelevant the conflict between the two parts of Ireland seemed to be in the overall context of a war-torn Europe. Far to the east he could see the sharp outline of the Giant's Causeway headland with the cliffs on the westernmost point of Rathlin Island beyond. His eye followed the coastline westwards past white cliffs and warm sandy beaches backed by high dunes. Consulting the map which lay open on chart table he identified the coastal towns of Portrush and Portstewart and he picked out the navigation light at the mouth of the River Bann. Across the mouth of the lough, less than a kilometre away he could clearly see the British Army patrol on Magilligan Point where the ferry from Greencastle used to dock. As he watched, one of the soldiers raised a pair of binoculars to his eyes and appeared to look directly at him. Karl had instinctively ducked out of sight before he realised the soldier was almost certainly just admiring the view of Donegal which rose steeply behind him. It must look beautiful in the the bright morning sunshine he thought. Looking due south and directly into the sun across the shimmering surface of the lough he could just make out the low-lying coastline of Northern Ireland above which loomed a high, black escarpment which he identified on the map as Benevenagh. He sighed deeply and slumped back into the skipper's seat behind the steering wheel wondering when he would next experience another moment of such peace and tranquility. One day perhaps when the war was over he thought he might return to this beautiful country and maybe even settle down.

Back in Harland and Wolff Pat was homing in on the most suitable place to plant the explosive. His team was applying modifications to the engine mounts after an overspeed engine test had produced serious vibrations at only marginally above what would be considered normal operation. Corvettes were fast vessels and often required maximum revs when hunting down submarines. As soon as the vibration issue was discovered it was immediately obvious it had to be fixed, not only in all the vessels currently under construction but retro fitted to those boats which were already in operation with the fault. The fix was straightforward in the corvettes in the earliest stage of production before the engine was fitted but for those with the engine already installed, fixing the problem involved some very tricky welding in almost inaccessible positions in the very bowels of the ship. It was a lengthy process which would take several weeks, affording Pat the opportunity to smuggle plastic explosives underneath the engine where it would not only destroy the engine but also blow a hole in the hull.

That night he received a call from Pearse, *'Pat, we have the goods now. The operation went without a hitch and I need to come and see you. My plan is to get dropped off at your house tomorrow evening around seven - after you get back from the shipyard. I'll not be in my Priest's outfit as it would look a bit out of place on Sandy Row! Anne has never seen me before so if she answers the door tell her I'll be wearing a hat and a mac and I'll be carrying a small suitcase - a bit like a door-to-door salesman. Keep a watch out for me so I don't have to hang around waiting for you to answer the door. It's best I'm not seen either coming or going. We'll need to spend a couple of hours to make sure you're au fait with everything. OK?'*

'Yes of course Pearse.' He replied, *'I'm keen to get on with the...'*

'We'll have plenty of time to get up to date tomorrow evening.' Pearse replied before immediately hanging up. Pat put the phone down, aware that he had been deliberately cut off before he could start talking about the operation. It felt like a rebuke. He briefed Anne and arranged that when Pearse arrived she would take her mother out for a drink as he preferred that she knew as little as possible about the project. When he kissed her goodnight later and retired as usual to the sofa he felt a ripple of excitement but the excitement wasn't about Operation Athchruthú, now it was exclusively about Anne and their future together. He just wanted to get the sabotage over and done with.

The following evening shortly after 7pm Pearse arrived at the door. Pat had been watching for his arrival and even before Pearse knocked, he'd swung the door open and greeted him. *'Good to see you Pearse. Come through to the kitchen. Anne and her mother are heading off to the pub and will be gone for a while.'* They exchanged pleasantries on the way out and when the two ladies had left the house the two IRA men sat down at the table where Pearse opened his suitcase.

'German plastic explosive is more or less the same as the gelignite we're familiar with - except it smells of almonds. I probably don't need to explain to you how to use it but as you can see it's in four long fat sausages which you can easily wrap into wherever you think it can cause the maximum damage. As far as getting them into Harland and Wolff I'll leave up to you but I suppose you could tie them around your waist or hang them from your belt and let them dangle down your

trouser legs...' He looked across at Pat as he spoke and grinned broadly, *'Might make you feel very manly, don't you think?'*

Pat then briefed Pearse on his current ideas about where to place the explosives, explaining that the timing was perfect because he and his specialist welding squad were currently applying the engineering change to the engine mounts. Furthermore, Pat had been assigned to fit the change to the next ship to be launched so if everything went according to plan, sabotaging it would block the entire production line for an indefinite period.

'Well done Pat,' said Pearse, *'but now we come to the tricky bit - how to detonate this German gelignite. Of course you could use an alarm clock but look what was contained in the shipment.'* At that he produced a tiny glass tube from his pocket and laid it on the table. To Pat it looked like a radio valve but inside the tube he could see what looked like a bead mercury. Pearse carefully lifted it up, keeping the terminals uppermost and then he gradually tilted it until the bead of mercury slid down the tube and over the ends of the contacts which were inside the valve. *'It's a tilt switch.'* He said as he handed it over to Pat. *'As soon as the mercury covers those contacts it completes the circuit and - Boom! Nifty isn't it? The problem with the alarm clock is first of all it ticks so anyone who happened to be nearby might hear it and second, an alarm clock will only last for at most twenty-four hours so to be safe you'd need to set it for less than twenty hours. I'm going to have to leave it up to you whether you use an alarm clock or find a way to use the tilt switch.'*

'I'll need to think about that but hopefully I can get it fixed in the next few days. As I said, the timing couldn't have been better. Now, would you like a dram before you leave? I've got a bottle of Jamieson's if you're interested?' Said Pat as he fetched a couple of glasses and the bottle from the kitchen cupboard.

'Personally I prefer Bushmills but Jamieson's will be fine thanks.' Replied Pearse, happy to find Pat in good spirits. *'Sláinte.'* He said, before downing the whiskey in a single gulp. *'Now tell me Pat, how are things going with Anne?'*

'Anne's a quare girl Pearse. She and her mother have been through hell and without the help of the IRA I don't know what they'd have

done.' Replied Pat, choosing to keep the depth of his feelings for Anne to himself for the time being. *'I'm still sleeping on the sofa, if that's what you're asking.'*

They made small talk until Anne and her mother returned from the pub and then on hearing his car arrive Pearse bade them goodbye and dashed down the steps into the back seat of the car. Pat took the suitcase into the lounge and placed it between the sofa and the wall with instructions to both ladies not to touch it under any circumstances. They understood precisely what that meant, the suitcase contained explosives. When Pat went to bed on the sofa that night, his head was only a few inches away from enough plastic explosives to blow up half the houses in the street. Even though he knew it was completely docile until triggered, it still kept him awake for a while as he considered how best to smuggle the German gelignite into Harland and Wolff. Once inside the yard he'd have to decide whether to hide it somewhere before placing it under the engine in the corvette, or take it directly to its final destination. He was also thinking about how to rig the detonator and whether to use the ingenious tilt switch or stick with the tried and tested alarm clock. One decision he did make before he drifted off was to share everything with Anne. This was in direct contravention of the orders he'd been given but that didn't take into account his life-changing event on Fair Head a few days ago. Now it was inconceivable that he could hide his purpose from the woman he intended to spend the rest of his life with. Not only did she deserve to know but she could also help him with more than just moral support, she could be a sounding board and help with practical things like how to hide the plastic explosive in his clothing. He longed to share the burden of his responsibility with Anne, just as he longed to share her bed but although her mother would have known they'd shared a bed in Ballycastle, it was a different story under her own roof. He had been tempted to ask Pearse to perform a quickie marriage in the house but that wouldn't have been right. He was only going to get married once and he wanted it to be a proper wedding, a special day which they and their friends would remember.

The following evening after supper Anne's mother went to bed early complaining of the beginnings of a head cold leaving the two of them alone in the sitting room in front of the crackling fire. He told her everything.

'I don't see how this can further the cause of Irish reunification, Pat. Collaborating with the Germans isn't going to make you many friends north or south of the border.' She said in a tone more resigned than challenging.

'The IRA is desperately short of arms and the only way we could rearm was doing a deal with the Germans. Although there are plenty of Irish-Americans who would give us guns and explosives, the war has shut off that supply channel completely. We've got the first shipment of arms from the Germans - a massive amount - and now we have to complete our side of the bargain before we get the second half. With these arms and explosives the IRA can become a fully functional, operational army again. Also, if the Germans win the war then this collaboration will stand us in good stead.' He responded defensively.

'So theoretically speaking, if you were to pull out of the operation it would only cost the IRA the second shipment?' She questioned gently.

'It would need to be a very convincing reason otherwise the Germans would think they'd been double-crossed. The IRA has few enough friends at the moment. Apart from the British, the Irish Government has cracked down on us in the hope that being nice to the Brits might deter them from invading us. Now if we upset the Germans we'd have no friends other than the Irish-Americans and they're not much use at the moment. It'd be great not to have to go through with this but I've no choice Anne, however I promise that this is my final IRA operation,' he paused for a moment before continuing, *'actually it's also my first. I've been a member of the IRA for years but believe it or not this is the first bit of active duty I've seen and I'll tell you straight Anne, I'm scared.'* He wanted to steer the discussion away from whether it was right or not but she wasn't having it.

'If you've no choice but to carry it through I hope you're not going to kill anyone in the process.' She said now in a more forceful voice.

'I'd already decided that.' He responded, squeezing her tightly. *'Time for bed now.'*

She looked at him with smiling eyes and said wistfully, *'When this is over, let's go away - as far away as possible from all the bigotry, anger and hatred. Let's find somewhere to live where nobody cares what religion we are.'*

They kissed and cuddled for a few moments before she broke away and headed for the door, turning to blow a final kiss to him as she pulled it shut. Tucking himself under the eiderdown he gazed vacantly into the dying embers of the fire and made a massive decision, come what may he would leave the IRA when this operation was over. It was often said amidst IRA circles that the only way to leave the organisation was in a box but that was patently not always true. If he could pull this operation off he'd be a hero within the ranks of IRA and surely they'd not ask more of him? He would never turn away from his fundamental belief in a united Ireland, it was simply that since he'd fallen in love with Anne his previous passion for the reunification of Ireland had now been supplanted totally by his determination to make a new life with the woman who had stolen his heart. But his immediate priority was to plant these explosives and finish the job. The next few days would be critical.

Pearse returned to his house where Karl and Liam were playing cards in the kitchen and chatting easily about the excitement of the arms shipment and how, even thought the transfer across Loch Foyle had been done more or less under the noses of the British troops stationed at Magilligan Point, it had gone without a hitch. Several trusted IRA men from Derry had been drafted in to help carry the arms across to Pearse's secret arsenal and as a reward each was given a bolt action Wehrmacht service rifle, the Mannlicher M1935, which was a most impressive weapon, vastly superior to the ancient Lee-Enfield WW1 rifles they'd been using since partition. Pearse couldn't have bought their loyalty more effectively in any other way - and he needed their loyalty. They now knew where the arsenal was hidden and if their loyalty had been questionable he'd have had to shoot them and made it look like they'd been murdered by the British.

'Right lads,' he said as he sat down at the table, *'all we can do now is wait. I don't see any need for either of you to stay in Belfast. For you Karl, the sooner you can get back to Dublin the safer you'll be and Liam, you'll have to drive him back down south. You've both done well and obviously I'll be back in touch once Pat has done his job. We can then start arranging for the second shipment.'*

'OK Pearse, we'll set off in the morning and head for Monaghan as usual,' replied Liam, 'will you get in touch with them to see which crossing we need to take?'

'Will do.' Said Pearse, well pleased with himself. He was now the most powerful man in the IRA and tomorrow he would brief the High Command from a position of strength. Some of them might be grumpy because he didn't inform them of the operation beforehand but he'd already decided that the second shipment of arms would have to go to the South which should keep them happy and fully occupied with arranging the second arms shipment from the Germans. Pearse now had what he needed to continue the armed struggle in the north with minimal interference from Dublin.

The following morning Liam and Karl said goodbye to Pearse and set off to drive back to Dublin. As before they avoided the main roads where it was almost certain they would encounter road blocks. The previous evening they'd got directions from Monaghan about which crossing to use and after a night back in the safe house they would be in Dublin the following day. For Liam life would return to something resembling normal and he was already looking forward to his first pint of Guinness in The Beggar's Bush. It had been quite an adventure but he was under strict instructions from Pearse not to reveal even the smallest detail of the operation. He'd have plenty of time during the drive to come up with a credible explanation for his lengthy absence. For Karl the job was only half done but in many ways it was the difficult half. The second shipment would almost certainly be landed somewhere in the south of Ireland so even if he was identified as having been involved in the process his diplomatic immunity would ensure that he wouldn't be charged. Then the worst that could happen to him would be deportation back to Germany. That might even mean promotion, he thought as the car trundled sedately through the Armagh countryside.

'I don't know about you Karl, but I'll be very glad to get back into Ireland,' said Liam as they approached the border, 'it's been a nerve-racking few weeks. I think a celebration will be in order when we get back to Dublin - don't you think?'

'Definitely a good idea Liam. I've acquired a taste for Guinness.' Replied Karl enthusiastically as they drove down a country lane bordered with high fuchsia hedges in fully bloom. *'Northern Ireland is very beautiful, especially the north coast. I will never forget the view along the coast towards the Giant's Causeway and one day when the war is over I am determined to come back and explore the area. Maybe there are as beautiful places in the southern Ireland?'* He queried, inviting Liam to educate him on some of the legendary Irish beauty spots. He'd barely completed the sentence when they rounded a blind bend in the road to see the thing they feared most, a British army roadblock only fifty yards ahead. Making an instant decision that with a German in the car they were doomed so he slammed on the brakes, crashed the car into reverse gear and accelerated hard back down the lane. They had a head start on the British but it was a race Liam was never going to win. With the engine screaming they were still only travelling at fifteen miles an hour while the British armoured scout car in pursuit was capable of sixty miles per hour. They were still a hundred yards ahead when they approached a sharp left hand bend in the road and for a few seconds Liam though they might just be able to escape across the fields if they rounded the corner, stopped the car, jumped the hedge and made a run for it. The border was less than a mile away and there was a slim chance they might make it. The plan was just coming together in his head when in mid-corner with his foot to the floor in reverse gear he lost control of the car and it tipped over on its side into the fuchsia hedge. He immediately fell out of his seat onto Karl pinning him to the door and they were still trying to disentangle themselves when the British scout car rounded the bend at high speed and finished the job off by ramming into the overturned car.

When Liam came around he was alone in a small cell with the worst headache he'd ever experienced in his life. This was bad, very bad. With considerable effort he sat up on the bed and held his head in his hands while he tried to come to terms with what had happened. Panic began to grip him as the enormity of his situation came home to him. This could mean indefinite incarceration in the Curragh or worse. Under pressure from the British the Irish Government had cracked down heavily on the IRA and simply being identified as a member of the organisation guaranteed detention and there were rumours of executions for those who had been involved in bombing campaigns.

There was no judicial process, no trial, no appeals process and virtually no hope of release. Then it hit him like a hammer blow to his already throbbing head - he was in Northern Ireland not the south. Detention had suddenly become the best he could hope for especially if his involvement in the sabotage operation and the arms shipment was discovered.

Unknown to Liam and in another cell Karl was also trying to come to terms with the dire situation he was in. He knew the British would immediately assume he was a spy and spies were shot. It was the same in Germany. The only possible protection a spy could hope for was if he or she was wearing an army uniform, which under the terms of the Geneva Convention might possibly mean being treated as a prisoner of war. His outlook was especially bleak. He wasn't wearing a Wehrmacht uniform and it would take very little effort to discover his true identity. After that his his fate would be sealed and it was only a question of when not if he'd be executed but his immediate concern was what might happen to him during the run-up to his execution. In Germany he knew that foreign spies were handled by the Gestapo. He also was well aware that suspected spies were interrogated to reveal the projects they were working on, the names of members of the resistance and the addresses of safe houses etcetera. He also assumed that in most cases interrogation meant torture and he had no reason to suppose that the British would handle a spy any differently. The best he could hope for would be to hold out until Pat could complete the mission. After that his time was up.

Then the door of his cell swung open and a British army officer came in and stood directly opposite him, *'Well Karl, would you care to explain what you've been doing in Northern Ireland?'* he asked politely while offering him a cigarette from a silver case. *'No thank you - I don't smoke,'* he replied, ignoring the question. The officer carefully extracted a cigarette from underneath their retaining elastic ribbon, snapped the case shut and after tapping it slowly and very deliberately on the back of the case he went through another studied ritual lighting it with a silver Zippo cigarette lighter. He then drew from it deeply before blowing the smoke out of his mouth and nose being careful turn away from Karl. Everything was done with style and was clearly intended to impress the prisoner. Fearful of what lay ahead but well in control of himself Karl noted that his captor was neither carrying a revolver not had any visible backup, although he assumed help was at hand should he decide to try to overcome the officer. It was obviously designed to put him at his ease, so he might lower is guard, but Karl maintained his composure and looked in silence back at the officer.

'I probably don't have to spell out to you the gravity of your situation but as a military attaché to the German embassy in Dublin, I think we can safely assume that your mission here was nefarious.' The officer said, enunciating every word and speaking slowly. Karl had no idea what the word 'nefarious' meant but it mattered little - he'd got the gist of what the officer had was saying, basically that his prospects weren't good. *'Seems like you're not in a talkative mood, Karl so I'll leave you to ponder this. You are a German spy, we are at war and like your country we execute spies. So the only interest we have in keeping you alive - for a while - is to learn from you what you were doing in Northern Ireland and who you were working with.'* He reached into the breast pocket of his jacket and pulled out a small pad of paper and a pen. *'Here Karl, you can write it all down while I'm away.'* He said with a slight nod of his head before turning smartly and headed for the door of the cell which, as if by magic, opened before him. Clearly there was a very attentive guard outside. Karl's mind raced as he turned over his options. Dreaming up a story which explained why he was in Northern Ireland was a non-starter so perhaps the best he could hope for was to stall for as long as possibly, thereby giving Pat the chance to complete the sabotage mission in Harland and Wolff. The army officer was obviously experienced at dealing with spies and he would know that news about Karl's capture would quickly leak out and whatever the operation he was involved in would either be rapidly advanced or postponed indefinitely. Karl had little choice but brace himself for some rough treatment in the next twenty-four hours, but he had no intention of betraying his IRA brothers-in-arms.

Meanwhile the army officer strolled down to Liam's cell where he went through the same performance but on this occasion Liam gratefully accepted the cigarette. *'Care to tell me why you were carrying a German spy as a passenger, Liam?'*

Liam said the first thing that came into his aching head, *'German spy? I don't know what you're talking about. I picked him up on the road out of Armagh - he was hitching a ride. I only realised he was a German when he got into the car.'*

'And where were you heading?' Questioned the officer politely.

'I'm heading back to Dublin after visiting friends in Belfast.' Responded Liam with growing desperation. He knew what was coming and he didn't have an answer.

'I see,' said the officer, *'perhaps you could tell me the name and address of the person you were visiting?'*

Aware that his story was becoming less and less plausible he replied, *'We met in a park somewhere, I can't remember which one.'*

The officer sighed theatrically, *'Liam, Liam, we can continue with this charade if you wish but you know and I know that it's a waste of our time. We were delivered a knee-capped body in the city yesterday - obviously one of yours. Our friends in the Irish Military Intelligence have identified him as Mick O'Reilly, a member of the IRA who was working for them. They knew it was only a question of time before he was exposed as a traitor, so his execution came as no surprise. In fact the signature knee-capping was unnecessary but that's presumably your way of deterring fellow members of the IRA from working for the government. Mick was a pal of yours wasn't he? So I think we can assume you're also a member of the IRA.'* The officer took a long drag on his cigarette and blew an immaculate smoke ring before continuing, *'Liam, you have to tell us what you are up to and who you're working with. We need to know.'* The officer then reached into the breast pocket of this jacket and handed a small pad and a pencil to Liam. *'I'll be back shortly.'* He said and smartly left the cell. Liam stared at the pad and considered his options none of which held the prospect of anything other than a lengthy spell of incarceration in the notorious Crumlin Road Gaol. However, one thing he knew for certain, if he shopped Pearse Kelly to the authorities he'd not have to endure a long spell in prison because he would be murdered, probably painfully, within days of being sent down. Such was the power and reach of the Belfast Battalion Commander in his home city.

When Liam and Karl failed to show up at the safe house in Monaghan alarm bells started ringing. Pearse was informed by phone and as soon as he received the news he immediately called Pat. *'This is the worst possible scenario Pat. We've got to assume that either Karl or Liam will spill the beans on us within a matter of days - maybe four at the most. That means if you're not able to plant the explosives in the next couple of days you've got to get out of there fast because if the British army come looking for you they will do so in force, the corvette production line is massively important to the British and they will go to any lengths to protect it. I will have to disappear straightaway so after this call Pat, you'll have to find your own way back to the South. Final word - it is possible that Karl and Liam will withstand interrogation and give nothing away, but it's not a risk worth taking.'*

'You said three or four days Pearse, right?' Questioned Pat.

'At most,' said Pearse, *'from what I know of the British interrogation methods they usually start slowly and let the prisoner sweat for a couple of days while they assess their resistance. If they think the prisoner is sitting on a lot of important information they won't hesitate to use torture but for the Brits that's usually a last resort. So yes, I think you can plan on three to four days but anything over that and you're taking a terrible risk. I think they'll give up on Karl quite quickly and just execute him. As a German spy he's going to die anyway whether he gives up some information or not. Liam's a different case. They will almost certainly find out that he's in the IRA and us dumping Mick's body outside the police station the other day won't have helped. If they learn from their counterparts in the South that he was an informer then it wouldn't be too difficult to trace his drinking pals in The Beggar's Bush. Once they discover Liam was one of Mick's friends he's done for. I doubt he'd be executed but he'll definitely spend a very long time in Crumlin Gaol. Personally I don't think he'll squeal because he knows if he did we'd find him and kill him whether he was inside the gaol or not. But all this is just guesswork. I'd work on getting the job done in three days at most or abandoning it - after all Pat, we've got the arms we needed. The corvette production line was the German target. Now that Karl is in the hands of the British Army it'll be obvious to the Germans that the plan has been blown.'*

'Christ Pearse this is dire. It means I'll have to plant the explosives tomorrow and then try to get out of Northern Ireland asap after that. Don't you think we need to give it a go otherwise the Germans will be pretty upset? We'd get no more arms from them and any future collaboration would almost certainly be out the window. And another thing Pearse, a successful operation of this scale would do wonders for our morale in the IRA and I'd say we need that.' Said Pat.

'Your call. I've given you my opinion.' Responded Pearse and immediately hung up.

It was now abundantly clear to Pat that he was on his own. Pearse's undisguised abandonment was a bitter pill to swallow as he'd been counting on his help to escape from Northern Ireland after the operation when for a while at least he'd be the most wanted man in the province. If either Karl or Liam squealed, whether or not his sabotage was successful wouldn't change his most-wanted status. He'd be on the run and what about Anne and her mother? They would also be tracked down as accomplices. That night he and Anne talked over the options. One was for the three of them to immediately make a run for the border but of course that would be a hazardous trip. The discovery of a German spy and a member of the IRA trying to cross the border would undoubtedly lead to more patrols. Obviously they couldn't stay in their house for more than another couple of nights at most so another option was to go into hiding somewhere and lie low until the hue and cry died down before making a bid to get across the border into the South. However, now that Pearse wasn't around to help they had no knowledge of safe houses so that option wasn't a starter. Then Pat had an idea.

'This is probably crazy but I think I should go ahead with the sabotage operation tomorrow because you never know, the Germans could well win this war and if they did they'd look favourably on us for helping them. Also, if I'm honest, the risk in setting it up is low. I have complete access to the engine room and for most of the time I'm alone. If I can get the explosives into Harland and Wolff I reckon it'll be straightforward to install them under one of the engines. The Germans have given me a thing called a tilt-switch which will detonate the explosive as soon as it's moved. That means that I can leave the ship and the yard and at some point in the future when the ship is launched or the engine started the explosives will automatically detonate.'

'And then what would we do Pat?' Said Anne with undisguised scepticism in her voice.

'Me not turning up for work the following day is bound to arouse suspicion and by then it's likely that one way or another the Brits will have got wind of the project, in which case they will be expecting me to head for the border as quickly as possible - that means South. What they won't be expecting is for us to head north - so that's what I'm proposing. The day after tomorrow instead of going into the shipyard, you and I can catch a bus up to the north coast, check-in to the Marine Hotel again and the following day start searching for somewhere off the beaten track to lie low.' He replied, warming to the idea even as he spoke.

'And what about my Mum?' She asked.

'She'd have to stay here. There's no way she could come with us and I don't think she's in any danger anyway. Even if the Brits turn up here she knows nothing about the operation and she'll know nothing about where we are. We can contact her later, when it's safe.'

'God Pat it's very scary - couldn't we sleep on it and decide tomorrow? Surely another day wouldn't make much difference?' She pleaded.

'We can't afford to waste any time Anne. I propose we go for this and only change the plan if something drastic happens tomorrow.'

'OK.' She said before pecking him on the cheek and heading upstairs to bed. When morning came they barely spoke as he dressed himself with the two long sausages of plastic explosive suspended from his belt and hidden in his trouser legs. The rest of the detonating equipment including the tilt-switch he was able to distribute in his pockets and lunch box. Pilfering from the shipyard was widespread and since joining the Harland and Wolff workforce it had been obvious that the security guards were less interested in what was being smuggled into the shipyard than in what might be smuggled out. By midday he'd hidden the explosives behind the engine mounts between the port engine and the hull. He had carefully taped the tilt-switch out of sight to the drive shaft thinking that when the corvette was launched the initial motion would trigger the explosion thereby blocking the production line until the damage to the hull and the engine could be made good. Even if the juddering as the ship slid down the slipway did not ignite the explosives, as soon as the engine was turned over for the first time, contact would be made and the explosion triggered. The ship was at most three days away from launching which would give him time to get out of the city with Anne and hide somewhere on the north coast.

Meanwhile in a military camp in Armagh Liam waited and waited, dreading what lay in store but weirdly impatient for them to get on with the interrogation however unpleasant it might prove to be. Of course this was their strategy he thought, make him sweat - and it was working. He had no idea how much time passed before the door suddenly swung open and in strode the dapper officer followed by two soldiers who without a word being spoken moved to either side of him and held his arms tightly. Again without speaking he was forced into the wooden chair which along with his bed were the only pieces of furniture in the cell. They tied him securely to the chair and withdrew to stand by the door. Then the officer spoke, *'Pat, I see you've not taken the opportunity to write anything down on the paper I left you yesterday so now's your last chance to tell me what you were working on and who you were working with. If you refuse then regrettably we'll have to do something which will loosen your tongue.'*

Liam remained silent and while looking straight at the officer his eyes delivered the message, *'Just get on with it.'*

The two soldiers returned to stand beside him again and as before they held him securely while the officer drew from his leather pouch a small syringe containing a clear liquid. He held it upwards and squirted a small amount of the contents out of the syringe to make sure it contained no air bubbles. *'Know what this is Liam?'* He said, *'I believe its proper name is sodium thiopental. It's still being developed but the scientists think it will encourage people like you to tell the truth. You're going to be the first guinea pig to try out this drug in Northern Ireland - you should feel honoured.'*

Liam watched in horror as one of the soldiers rolled up his sleeve and the officer injected the contents of the syringe into the bulging vein near his elbow. Seconds later he began to feel slightly drowsy and within minutes he felt as if he was sliding into a twilight world on the edge of oblivion. A questioning voice entered his head and he heard himself talking as though it were someone else. He could hear the conversation like a member of the audience at a theatrical production, it wasn't painful or unpleasant but it was extremely disquieting because he had lost control.

When the interrogating officer eventually returned to Karl's cell he had what looked like a satisfied smile on his face. Karl had no idea how much time had passed or whether it was day or night as his cell had no window to the outside and the light had been on continuously since he arrived. His watch had been removed on arrival and his passport and other papers had been confiscated. Finally he'd had his shoes and belt removed.

'Good day Karl,' he said 'I have good news and bad news - good news for us and the bad news for you. Your IRA colleague has been very cooperative indeed so we now know everything about your collaboration with the IRA, the arms shipment and the plan to sabotage the Harland and Wolff shipyard. In a way I suppose this is also good news for you because now you will be spared - how can I put this - the harsher interrogation methods which might have been necessary. However, the bad news is that you are to face a military court tomorrow morning and if as seems inevitable you are convicted of being a spy, you will be executed. Cigarette?' He said, as he opened his silver cigarette case and extended it towards Karl who replied, 'I don't smoke, sir, I always believed it wasn't good for my health.'

'Excellent!' Responded the officer, 'and who says the Germans don't have a sense of humour? Auf wiedersehen Karl, you are a brave man and I salute you.' The officer briefly clicked his heels and swung the cell door closed behind him. Left alone in the silence he knew he had at most twenty-four hours to live and there was nothing, absolutely nothing he could do about it. As he sat there idly gazing around this sparse cell, numb from what he'd just heard the strangest of thoughts came into his head. He remembered a story that had been doing the rounds in Berlin about the Great Depression in the United States. One of the major New York newspapers launched a writing competition where budding authors were provided with the first paragraph of a story which they were asked to complete. Entries were to be judged by a panel of famous American writers and the winner would receive the princely sum of $1,000, a fortune in those times. The starter paragraph described the predicament of a prisoner like him, locked in a cell with no windows but into which was pouring a torrent of water. The level of the water quickly rose until the poor prisoner was treading water with his head pressed hard against the ceiling and with only a rapidly diminishing space of air to breathe his situation could hardly have been worse. The newspaper was overwhelmed with submissions, the longest of which ran to five hundred pages but it was the shortest submission of them all which was chosen as the winner. That author had completed the story with a single sentence - *'With one bound he was free.'*

Karl looked around his cell and up to the ceiling and then burst into a bout of uncontrolled laughter. On hearing the laughter the guard outside the cell opened the tiny peephole in the door and looked in to see the condemned German spy in near-hysterics. *'Strange people the Germans.'* He muttered to himself as he shut the peephole. The following day Karl was convicted of being a German spy in time of war and summarily executed by firing squad at dawn the following day.

At the end of his shift Pat left the shipyard for the last time and walked back to the house on Sandy Row where Anne greeted him with a huge bearhug, *'I'm so relieved you're back safely Pat, how did it all go?'* She said as she led him through to the kitchen where her mother had brewed a pot of tea. *'I've told Mum that you and I have to go away for a while and she's fine with that, aren't you Mum?'*

Grace looked across at Pat with sad eyes and spoke softly, *'I don't know what you're up to Pat and I don't want to know, but whatever it is, I hope this - time away - is a sign that it's all over. Don't worry about me. The IRA have looked after me since your father was murdered and I know they will continue to look after me when you're gone. You have your lives to live and the last thing I'd ever want is to be a burden so please do what's right for you and don't worry about me, I'll be fine.'*

Dinner that evening was a very quiet affair and after tidying away the dishes Pat said, *'I think we ought to go down to McHugh's as usual for a pint, what do you say Anne? We'll be off in the morning so it might be a while before we're back there again.'*

'*We're all packed up so - yes, I think it's a grand idea. But we'll have to be careful not to behave differently.*' She replied with a slight movement of her head and raised eyebrows. She was warning him he mustn't drop his guard.

'*One pint only Anne, I promise.*' He responded, getting the message.

McHugh's was busier than usual that night. It turned out to be one of the regular's birthday so no sooner had they crossed the threshold than two celebration pints for them were ordered by the birthday boy. A small Irish trio was playing folk music in the corner and the air was filled with smoke, loud conversation and singing. It was hard to believe that the world was at war. They joined their friends at the usual table sequestering a couple of seats from an adjacent table while a young couple were dancing a jig on the tiny parquet dance floor in front of the trio. The entire pub throbbed with vibrancy and joy. Pat couldn't help thinking of the explosive charges he'd placed in the bowels of the corvette and he shuddered to think that when they went off, one of these great people might be hurt. They joined in but their hearts had already departed so it wasn't long before Pat made their excuses and got up to leave, ordering their round on the way out.

Hand-in-hand they walked in silence back towards the house. It was a dark night with a strong wind blowing ragged clouds across a crescent moon. '*I'll miss our new friends Anne. Since I've been here I've realised how alike we all are irrespective of whether we're from the north or the south, or whether we're Catholic or Protestant. We're brought up to be what our parents are and by the time we can speak we've already become bigoted. We get it in our mother's milk.*'

Anne was about to reply when the mournful wail of an air raid siren interrupted their peaceful walk. Soon the rumble of German bombers filled the night and searchlights stabbed the sky. A couple of anti-aircraft guns opened up but it felt like an inadequate response to what appeared to be a massive raid on the city. '*They'll be targeting the shipyard,*' Said Pat, '*we need to get as far away from the docks as we can!*' They broke into a run towards the house which lay in the opposite direction from the shipyard but a series of massive explosions up ahead brought them to a sudden stop. *'Oh my God, Pat, they're bombing the city!'* Anne cried out in horror, *'Mum will be terrified - we need to hurry.'*

All hell broke loose as wave after wave of German bombers dropped their deadly payloads across Belfast leaving the city ablaze as fires erupted from the flattened buildings. The sirens of fire-engines, ambulances and police added to the cacophony of sound that assaulted them as they ran back to the house, directly towards the firestorm as the bombers thundered ominously overhead and passed out across the shipyard and over Belfast Lough. As they rounded the corner an apocalyptic landscape of destruction and death lay ahead. What had been their terrace of houses had been reduced to a long ragged pile of burning rubble. A single fire engine was hopelessly attempting to douse the flames while beyond lay a city in flames. The war had finally come to Belfast and the city had been almost totally unprepared. Soon the sound of the bombers faded and the air raid siren ceased its awful moaning cry but above the sirens of the rescue vehicles the crackling sound of burning timbers filled the night and waves of ash-laden heat from the fires kept them at bay where they stood in shock. *'Nobody could survive that.'* Said Pat. Before Anne could respond a policeman on the other side of the road yelled across at them, *'Go to the school - back there!'* he said, gesturing wildly in the direction of the secondary school, *'Everyone is to assemble in the school. Food and blankets will be delivered there soon. Now go!'* They made their way back down the road and joined the growing throng of people streaming towards the school in a river of frightened humanity. When they found a quiet corner of the gym they sat down and he held her in his arms as she sobbed quietly. *'She's dead isn't she Pat?'*

'Yes.' He replied as tenderly as he could but nothing he could say or do could alleviate her grief. Finally her sobbing stopped, *'And these are the people you've been collaborating with? How do you feel about that now Patrick McGonigle? How many innocent people have they murdered in Belfast tonight?'* He had no answer. All he could do was to hold her tightly as the room slowly filled with the broken, sobbing survivors of the air raid. In time she dozed off but there was no sleep for him as he tried to work out what to do. There was no doubt whatsoever that Anne's mother was dead and it might be weeks before the bodies

that were buried beneath the rubble were discovered, by which time they would already be decomposing. His first thought was to volunteer to help the rescue services but it was quickly extinguished by his natural instinct to flee. He wanted to run away from the horror of the death and destruction and he also wanted to run away from the British Army. They would be coming after him just as soon as they forced either Liam or Karl to squeal.

It then hit him like a hammer blow to the head - if the British Army came looking for him they would learn that he and Anne had left the pub shortly before the air raid and had headed back to the house which they would find in ruins and assume that they'd perished inside. Would they bother to search the ruins to confirm he was dead? Most unlikely, he concluded. This tragedy could be a blessing in disguise. When dawn came he gently explained to Anne that they should head for York Street Station and catch a train to Portrush on the north coast. They were refugees now and they had to go somewhere. *'I'm sure the good folk of North Antrim will help us and while we're safe up there we can work out how to get back into the Free State.'*

As they prepared to leave the school the BBC News was broadcast throughout the classrooms. It had been a terrible night for Belfast. The raid had killed more than five hundred citizens and the death toll was still rising, many more were injured. Destruction in the city was massive but only two bombs were reported to have landed on the shipyard so all employees were advised to turn up for work as usual. On hearing the solemn BBC announcer, Pat realised it was the first time he'd thought about the explosives he'd planted since they'd been to the pub the previous night. Idly he wondered if a German bomb had perhaps landed on or near the corvette in which he'd laid the charges and triggered the explosion? But he no longer cared. Their world had been turned upside down and everything had changed. Now all he wanted to do was to find a quiet place where he and the woman he loved could start their life together in peace, far, far away. He wanted nothing more to do with the IRA or the Germans or the war.

The emergency services served tea and rolls to everyone in the school and while they were eating, word was passed around that anyone who had lost their home and had nowhere to go would be looked after in Portrush while they sorted their lives out so when they'd finished eating they set off to walk to York Street Station. They had only the clothes they stood up in as suitcase that Anne had carefully packed for them was now buried underneath tons of rubble in the remains of their house. Fortunately Pat had almost a full week's wages in his wallet so they should have enough to survive for a few days when the charity ran out. Already a plan was forming in Pat's head about how to escape to the South but for the moment his priority was to comfort Anne as she grieved for the tragic loss of her mother. The walk to York Street Station took nearly an hour and on the way they passed many more bomb-damaged scenes of destruction and death. Up to now the war had been something that was happening elsewhere, the blitz was confined to London and the other major cities in England but no longer. The war had arrived in Belfast and they were in the midst of it. The station was busy, mostly with people like them, refugees with nothing. Gaunt faces, many still covered in the dust and debris of the aftermath of the bombing, acknowledged them with understanding and compassion. Nobody spoke but the air was filled with the quiet sounds of grief.

An hour later a train backed into the station and they climbed into a compartment along with a family of four who like them had lost everything including their house and their parents. Anne spend most of the two hour journey with her head resting on his shoulder while across the compartment the family sat motionless and silent for the entire journey, the children looking out of the windows while their parents held hands and dozed fitfully as the train chuffed its way northwards. It was mid-afternoon when the train lurched into the small seaside town station and they disembarked onto the platform with the smell of the sea filling their nostrils. Members of the town council met them at the station exit where they were split into groups of five and six and taken past the Town Hall down Kerr Street to a row of boarding houses which had been commandeered to provide temporary accommodation for the fifty or so homeless refugees who had chosen to leave Belfast for Portrush. Towns all over Northern Ireland were providing support in an upwelling of community spirit which for once wasn't defined by religion. The bombs didn't discriminate between Catholics and Protestants.

Pat and Anne were shown to an attic room on the third floor overlooking the harbour and after a light supper prepared by the landlady they returned to their bedroom and the sat together on the end of the bed for a few minutes watching the sun spill molten gold over the Donegal hills, only twelve miles away along a glimmering, golden pathway across the sea. Emotionally drained and physically exhausted they climbed into the bed and snuggled down under the blankets quickly falling asleep in each others arms.

Over breakfast the following morning the BBC somberly announced the dreadful statistics of Belfast's dead and injured but quickly moved on to emphasise the spirit of defiance exhibited by both communities and the upwelling of anger at the German bombers who had callously and deliberately bombed civilian areas in the city. The newsreader faintly mocked the German pilots for only managing to land two bombs on the shipyard, one landed in the water and the other inflicting minor damage on a corvette which was nearing completion. Everything was already back up and running as normal in the shipyard and the workers were more motivated than ever to build the ships which protected the north Atlantic convoys from the U-boat wolf-packs. Pat looked across at Anne with raised eyebrows and nodded his head. *'It's great there were no casualties in the shipyard.'* He said. Anne knew what he meant - his explosives had almost certainly been triggered by the solitary German bomb that dropped on the shipyard. For a while they ate in silence but Pat wasn't listening to the news, he was thinking that perhaps when the Germans had learnt that Karl and Liam had been captured trying to cross the border into Southern Ireland they assumed the operation had been called off, leaving them with the only other option of launching a massive air raid. It seemed to make sense but the more he thought about it the more he realised he no longer cared. Reaching across the table he took both of Anne's hands in his and looking into her eyes he said softly, *'You've no idea how much I love you Anne. This is day one of the rest of our lives so let's start planning our future together and never look back.'* Anne smiled broadly and squeezed his hands tenderly, she had no need to speak, Pat could see the love in her eyes and feel the embrace in her touch. *'Let's go for a walk, it looks like being a beautiful day.'*

A short while later they were sitting at the outermost point of the harbour's north pier looking across at the sweep of the West Strand which stretched between the harbour and the cliff-bound coastline which lay to the west. The golden strand was backed by soft dunes clad in stiff bent grass and behind the dunes on the railway viaduct a train was pulling slowly out of the station on its journey to Belfast. The harbour was quiet and the local fishing boats they'd seen from their window in the B&B the previous evening had departed to the fishing grounds. All that was left were a line of punts which lay on running moorings from the shore and several sailing boats moored to brightly coloured buoys. The steamer had also left and a huge conical pile of coal was gradually being shovelled onto lorries. For a long time they said nothing and then Anne leant her head on Pat's shoulder and whispered, *'Are we safe here Pat?'* She could read his thoughts. Ever since they'd arrived in the town this question had been uppermost in his mind but he had no way of knowing.

'We're safe for a few days - I'm sure of that, but if either Liam or Karl have been turned, then the Brits will definitely come after me. They'll quickly find out that I've not shown up at the shipyard since the air raid and that we were drinking in McHugh's before it all kicked off. Any one of our friends would have told them that we'd left the pub and probably been killed in the raid but once the rubble was cleared and only one body found - your mother's - then they will continue to search for me. They'll also know that the damage to the corvette couldn't have been done by a German bomb dropped from the air, it could only have been done by explosives placed at the bottom of the ship. They'll definitely be trying to find me and also desperately searching for Pearse's arms cache. The fact that this operation was a collaboration with the Germans will have incensed the Brits.' He sighed deeply before continuing, *'Right now the rescue services will be frantically searching for bodies in the ruins in the hope of finding some that are still alive. If they only discover your mother's body then.....they'll know an IRA bomber is still at large.'*

'You're scaring me Pat,' she said, lifting her head from his shoulder and looking straight at him. *'What would they do to you if they caught you?'*

'Thinking about that gets us nowhere Anne, it's a waste of time. We need to concentrate on how to get over there.' He said, pointing at Donegal which was brightly illuminated by sunshine and in the clear air seemed deceptively close. 'Look, about half way up the coast towards Malin Head there's a small village called Culdaff with a beautiful beach beneath it. You can't see the beach from here but it's one of only two breaks in the cliffs all the way up that coast line. Culdaff beach can't be more than twenty miles away. We could practically swim there... Greencastle is even closer - twelve miles at most. There, do you see where the sweep of Magilligan Strand ends? That's the mouth of Lough Foyle and just across from it you can see the lighthouse which is just up the road from Greencastle. The problem with trying to get there is that it's just a hundred yards or so from from the military post in Northern Ireland and the British army can see everything that's going on in Greencastle, almost without using binoculars. We could easily be intercepted and detained.' His reply expressed most of his fears but he spared her his doubts about their safety in Southern Ireland. Collaborating with the Germans would undoubtedly have incensed the British and they will have increased the pressure on the Irish Government to clamp down even harder on the IRA. The precarious Irish neutrality meant balancing relations between Britain and German in the knowledge that if they got it wrong, either Britain or Germany could invade Ireland in days. At other times the IRA could feel relatively safe in Southern Ireland but now they ran the risk of spending years in internment without trial. While there was no doubt that he would have more friends in the South, the price paid by ordinary citizens for harbouring members of the IRA was high. Also, he was aware that if his name was known to the Irish Military Intelligence it was unlikely he could ever return to his job at the Steam Packet Company. Their best hope was that they would be reported as missing, assumed dead, but that wasn't a risk he felt he could take. So as they sat there at the end of the pier, he turned over in his mind how they might be able to make it to Donegal where they could at least hide out in Buncrana for a while.

The sun warmed then and for a long time there was a comfortable silence between them. Everything seemed so peaceful and in such contrast to what they had witnessed only a short time ago in Belfast -

the harbour, the town, the railway station, the amusement park, the beach, the dunes the cliffs, the sea everything in sight was as it always had been - normal. However beneath the surface was a growing anxiety about the war and its consequences. Rationing was harsh and many hitherto common items were no longer available but life went on.

'It would be nice to live here, don't you think?' Said Pat eventually.

'You're not serious, are you?' Responded Anne turning to look at him, her stern expression making no attempt to disguise her impatience, *'I think we need to concentrate totally on how we're going to get to Donegal. You're a sailor, couldn't we take one of those boats and sail across? As you've said, it's not far.'*

'That's probably our best option but you've never sailed before and I'm not sure I could handle one of those yachts on my own, especially getting it out of the harbour. However, it's a good idea Anne - we need to give it some serious thought. Thanks for bringing me back to reality, I guess I'm a typical bloody Irishman - a dreamer.' He smiled and kissed her gently on her forehead, in a flash realising he was being selfish. Anne had just lost her mother and he was behaving almost as if nothing had happened. *'Time I started thinking more about the woman I love - let's go for a stroll along the strand and decide how many children we're going to have.'* He said.

'We've a lot do before we get around to that!' She replied cheerfully as she dragged him to his feet. *'How many children we're going to have can wait but we definitely need to talk about what we do next.'*

That evening over tea in the B&B they listened intently to the BBC News. The headlines were still dominated by the aftermath of the air raid and the death toll had risen to over eight hundred with almost twice that number injured. The announcer didn't mince words and described the destruction in the city as apocalyptic and even Crumlin Gaol, not far from the shipyard had received a direct hit allowing several prisoners to escape. Most were rounded up within hours and a number of them, knowing that that their recapture was inevitable, had headed straight to the nearest bar where, the announcer lightly commented, they were allowed to finish their drinks before being herded into the waiting Black Marias. Finally he emphasised that *'the spirit of the people remained undiminished'* which seemed unlikely to Pat but maybe the reality of war would have some positive consequences and for some strange reason he wondered if the amount of stolen goods being smuggled out of Harland and Wolff would reduce.

Meanwhile Anne barely heard the news. The loss of her mother and leaving her buried in the ruins of their home was overwhelming her with guilt. While other daughters were digging in the rubble with their bare hands in the hope of finding their mothers alive, she had looked at what was left of their house and then walked away. Although she knew she could do nothing about it now she also knew in her heart that this guilt would be with her for life.

Before turning in that night, Pat spent a long time standing at the window looking at the yachts in the harbour. He could see no other option than to steal one of the boats and try to sail to Donegal. His preferred choice was an elegant gaff sloop with an open cockpit which would take a crew of four with ease. It looked fast and seaworthy but it would be quite a handful to sail singlehanded. The other possibility was an attractive clinker-built dingy with a Bermudan rig about fourteen feet long. Although it was clearly designed for a crew of two and he felt confident he could handle it on his own, however it was very small for a twenty-mile open water passage across in the North Atlantic and far too risky in anything but ideal weather conditions, he concluded. Irrespective of which boat he chose, getting away from the harbour unnoticed would be difficult and even if they did manage to leave unseen, what if the lifeboat was launched to give chase? His train of thought was interrupted with a timely invitation to come to bed. *'Are you going to spend all night staring out of the window?'* She questioned sleepily.

It was a troubled night for Pat tossing and turning as he fretted about how to get across the border and back into Southern Ireland. Stealing a boat seemed like the best and maybe the only option but which boat? He could see that the larger yacht had its sails rigged and ready to hoist but there was no sign of the sails for the clinker dinghy. They could have been stored below the foredeck but equally the owner could easily store the sails at home and carry them to the boat for each outing. That's what he'd do but the only way to be sure would be to row out to the dinghy and check. This would have to be done in a dead of night and if he was spotted slipping out of the B&B it would raise suspicions. For all he knew his description might be in the process of being circulated around the hostels and B&Bs which were providing accommodation for the Belfast refugees. He'd foolishly given their names to the council when they'd arrived on the train so if either Karl or Liam had revealed his identity under interrogation then it wouldn't be long before the British found him. He cursed himself for not giving false names - a careless slip-up which could prove fatal. They had no identification now as both their passports were buried under tons of bricks in the ruins of Anne's house so they could have chosen any names they'd wanted. By the time the first rays of sun were hitting the black cliffs at the west end of the stand he'd made up his mind that this had to be their final day in Portrush. With every day that passed their risk of being discovered increased dramatically so that night after dark they would have to borrow one of the punts which were lying on running moorings and row it out to the sailing boat, but which one? It all depended on the weather but if it was suitable to take the dinghy he had no way of knowing if its sails stowed on board. Finally he decided that if the weather looked ok they would row first to the clinker dinghy and if the sails were on board then they'd take it. If the sails weren't on board then he'd have no choice but to take the larger day-boat and hope that he could safely manoeuvre it out of the harbour by himself. Once out in the open sea he felt that sailing conservatively they should be OK although he was far from sure where and how to come ashore in Donegal. But they had to get there before he needed to worry about that.

Over breakfast he explained his plan to Anne who had nothing to add. *'Wish I could be of more help but I've never been in a sailing boat before so I haven't a clue. It'll also be pitch dark so please don't ask me to do anything complicated!'* She said, trying to lighten the mood a little.

After they'd eaten they walked along the South Pier of the harbour and picked out the lightest punt they could use to get to the yachts which were lying on swinging moorings in the middle of the harbour. He felt bad about having to steal a boat from a town which had shown such generous hospitality to them but he thought that maybe he could leave message on it if they arrived safely in Donegal and it might even get returned? However this was very faint hope, he wasn't planning to sail the stolen yacht into Greencastle which was the only harbour within reach. Secretly he knew he'd almost certainly have to beach the yacht and scramble ashore. *'You can swim, can't you Anne?'* He questioned in as casual a voice as possible. Seeing Anne's startled look he quickly added, *'Don't worry. We won't be doing any swimming, I just thought I should know....'*

'I can't.' she replied with concern filling her face, *'Swimming wasn't something anyone bothered about when I was growing up.'*

'I'm sure there'll be life jackets on board anyway so no need to worry.' He replied as confidently as he could manage. Feeling the need to boost her confidence he said, *'The weather is ideal at the moment. This southerly wind should make it easy to get out of the harbour and then we'll be on a reach the whole way which should make for a fast passage. When the wind is offshore like this the sea is flat which means we'll travel faster and drier. If we get away around midnight and the wind holds, we should be arriving off the coast of Donegal around dawn. The only worry I have is that the wind might die away at night as it sometimes does with a southerly. However, that's in the lap of the Gods and there's no point in worrying about it. One other thing, we could do with some waterproofs. It will get cold at night and it might also get a bit wet. Let's head into town and see if we can buy some wet weather gear. I've still got most of my last wage packet so we should be ok.'*

Anne was having difficulty controlling her fear but she was determined not to show weakness to Pat who had enough to worry about without her getting weak at the knees. All she could do was to keep telling herself that tomorrow morning the would be safe in Donegal and beyond the reach of the British Army. One of Pat's friends would come and pick them up and if everything went to plan they could be safe in Buncrana in twenty-four hours. It hardly seemed plausible but this was a psychological lifebelt that she clung to with all her might.

It was early afternoon and the town was busy with people going about their everyday business when they found an outdoor shop which sold waterproof clothing, quickly outfitting themselves with long waterproof coats and sou'westers. *'Expecting bad weather?'* Said the shopkeeper making conversation. *'I hope not,'* said Pat with feeling, *'but it's better to be prepared.'*

Carrying their new purchases they exited onto the busy Main Street and almost collided with a man who was hurrying past the entrance to the shop. Regaining his balance Pat apologised, *'So sorry, I wasn't looking where I was....'* but the sentence remained unfinished and he froze to the spot staring wide-eyed at the man he had collided with - it was Liam O'Donnell, his IRA colleague who had been captured by the Brits and who almost certainly had betrayed both him and Pearse.

'Pat,' he said, *'We need to talk. I can explain if you give me the chance.'*

Anne came to Pat's rescue by pointing across the road to a café and saying, *'You have obviously some catching up to do so why don't we go over there and get something to drink?'*

They found a quiet table near the back of the café and ordered a pot of tea which Anne poured while the air crackled with electricity between the two men. In a hushed voice Pat looked at Anne and said, *'This is Liam O'Donnell, you've heard me mention his name a lot recently. He was captured by the Brits along with the German and it was either Liam here or the German who betrayed us.'*

Over the next half hour Liam told the story of how he was injected with a 'truth drug' and hadn't been aware of what he'd told them. But he was't denying that it was probably him and not the German who spilled the beans on the sabotage plan, his reasoning being that he wasn't subjected to any torture and so he assumed that under the influence of the drug he had told them everything they wanted to know. *'I don't know what happened to Karl but they probably shot him. If I'd told them all they wanted to know, there'd be no point in keeping him alive. They sent me to Crumlin Gaol and during the air-raid a bomb blew a hole in the wall of our wing and I and most of my cellmates escaped. I hitched a lift in an animal transporter to Coleraine and I've just come down here in the hope that I can find somewhere to hide. The B Specials, the police and the army will all be looking for me and I'll be honest with you Pat, I've not got long to live anyway because I know Pearse is looking for me as well. If the Bs find me first they'll send me back to jail where it was already common knowledge what I did. I'm sure that was deliberately leaked. One day there'll be 'an accident' and I'll be* found dead. The screws won't care - in fact they'll probably turn a blind eye. I'm a dead man walking Pat.'

'You'll get what you deserve Liam. I can't see Pearse buying the 'truth drug' story. My first instinct is to shop you but we're on the run also.' Said Pat trying to suppress the feeling of pity which was growing inside him. Liam had confessed that it was probably him who had given the game away when he could just as easily said it was the German. It made his story more plausable. Then glancing across at Anne as if to seek her approval he proceeded to tell Liam in detail what they were planning. Anne was not surprised, she knew instantly what was going through Pat's mind - Liam was a potential crew.

'Have you ever done any sailing Liam.' Said Pat.

'A long time ago when I was at school we used to sail dinghies at Howth on Saturdays. I know the basics - does this mean you'd take me with you?' He replied with the first detectable lift in his voice since they'd met.

'We're leaving tonight Liam. Meet us at the bathing huts on the South Pier of the harbour at 11pm if you want to come.' Pat said as he got to his feet to leave. Anne looked at him and then at Liam and her heart leapt when she saw both men simultaneously extend their hands to shake as friends once more.

As they made preparations to slip out of the B&B that evening Anne said, 'I'm glad you made it up with Liam. I feel sorry for him now - he's not safe anywhere, here in Northern Ireland, in Southern Ireland and even in jail. He seems to have resigned himself to having only a short time to live.'

'I believe him but Pearse will never buy the truth drug story. He's already executed Mick for working for Irish Intelligence so he'll not hesitate to execute Liam when he catches up with him. Liam has no friends on earth other than us at the moment so I'd be amazed if he didn't turn up tonight. I really hope he does. We're going tonight come what may but it would certainly help to have another hand on board, especially as he's done some sailing before. It's like riding bike, if you learn how to sail when you're young you never forget it.' Said Pat with feeling.

'Do you think he'll ever find peace, Pat?' She replied.

'*Peace - how I look forward to you and me having some peace! Come here,*' he said with his arms open wide.

They hugged for a long time and he whispered in her ear,

I will arise and go now, and go to Innisfree,
And a small cabin build there, of clay and wattles made;
Nine bean-rows will I have there, a hive for the honey-bee,
And live alone in the bee-loud glade.

And I shall have some peace there, for peace comes dropping slow,
Dropping from the veils of the morning to where the cricket sings;
There midnight's all a glimmer, and noon a purple glow,
And evening full of the linnet's wings.

I will arise and go now, for always night and day
I hear lake water lapping with low sounds by the shore;
While I stand on the roadway, or on the pavements grey,
I hear it in the deep heart's core.'

'*My goodness!*' she exclaimed, '*That was beautiful! You're full of surprises Patrick McGonigle.*'

He smiled and squeezed her tightly, '*I can't think of anything that better describes peace. It's a poem by William Butler Yeats which I learnt at school and never forgot. Tell you what - let's go to the Lake Isle of Innisfree one day, what do you say?*'

'*Definitely!*' She replied.

Nobody saw them slip out of the B&B at five to eleven and once outside they stole quietly and quickly across the road and down the ramp to the South pier. As they neared the bathing huts a figure emerged from the shadows and greeted them. '*Which punt do you want to take?*' he questioned, '*only a few of them have oars on board and I reckon the small one over there is best.*'

'*Thanks Liam, let's take it.*' Replied Pat, grateful that Liam was already actively contributing.

A few minutes later they were clambering on board the yacht. Liam attached the punt's painter to the mooring buoy while Pat hoisted the mainsail as quickly and as quietly as possible.

'*I'll sail her out of the harbour under the main and we can hoist the jib when we're outside in the bay. Cast her off when you're ready Liam,*' whispered Pat who was standing by the helm with Anne sitting on the side deck beside him. A soft southerly breeze wafted them safely past the small navigation light on the tip of the North Pier and out into the open sea. It was a dark night with almost complete cloud cover but in the distance Pat picked up a light which he assumed was from the lighthouse on Inishowen. He pointed it out to Anne while Liam hanked on the jib and hoisted it, *'We need to aim to the right of that light Anne and when we close the land we have to follow the coastline until we find a beach we can land on. Conditions are great at the moment and if they stay the same for the next three or four hours the wind will be offshore at Inishowen so there shouldn't be any drama beaching the yacht.'*

Once under full sail the yacht picked up speed but before he could relax he felt a stronger gust of wind coming from just forward of the beam. Hoping that this was not a sign of a change in the weather Pat said nothing as he hardened in on the mainsheet while Liam tightened in the jib. They were still laying their course but if the wind veered much more it would be a worry, however progress was good and they had got clear away without attracting any unwanted attention.

Steering without a compass Pat tried to hold a course directly towards the Inishowen light but this became increasingly difficult as the wind continued to veer around into the southwest. He was already hard on the wind with the sheets pinned in while the three of them sat out on the weather deck trying to keep the yacht as upright as possible. Fortunately the sea remained reasonably calm and progress was good. *'She's a fine yacht,'* said Pat, *'we must be averaging between four and five knots and the closest beach I'm aiming for can't be more than fifteen miles from Portrush - so we should be there before dawn but hopefully there'll be enough light for us to see what we're doing.'*

Choosing to keep his concerns about the veering wind to himself he held a course as high to the wind as possible. He hadn't been sailing for many years but the thrill of feeling the boat respond when the sails were perfectly tuned had him adjusting the mainsheet on an almost continuous basis. Liam was also kept on his toes with a continuous stream of 'in-a-bit', 'out-a-bit' instructions from Pat. Anne was between them trying to come to terms with the huge changes that had swept through her life in the previous few days. She'd fallen in love with an IRA bomber who was being hunted by the British Army, she'd lost her mother and her home in an devastating German air-raid, become a refugee and was now in a stolen boat far out at sea in the middle of the night trying to escape to the relative safety of the South. Was she afraid? A bit perhaps but deep inside she felt the delicious thrill of excitement as a new horizon in her life beckoned. She was still grieving the death of her mother but in her heart she felt certain that her mother would forgive her for the choice she'd made. Now she owed it to her mother to make the most of every day and live life to the full. Their flight to Donegal was the first leg of a lifelong journey in search of a new horizons and new experiences, the core ingredients of a fulfilling and satisfying life.

'Right lads, is it breakfast in Buncrana then?' She said with a broad grin on her face. Liam laughed and replied, *'My mouth is already watering at the thought of a celebration Ulster fry - one you could hardly lift.'* It was the first time she'd heard him laugh, let alone smile. What did the future hold for him, she wondered?

As the night wore on the wind freshened and continued to veer bit by bit into the south west. Pat could no longer lay the lighthouse and was beginning to worry that the wind might swing all the way around to the west, forcing them to beat up to the shore at Inishowen. That would take longer but in some ways it would help because a westerly wind would be more directly offshore, sheltering their approach and ensuring there were no rollers coming up onto the beach where he intended to run aground. The dinghy would have helped them land but towing it behind them would have added drag and taken at least a knot off their speed so now they had no option other than to run the yacht up on the beach and leap ashore. He felt bad about stealing the yacht and even worse about abandoning it on the beach when they landed. One day when this was all over he thought it would be nice to return to Portrush and compensate the owner for the loss of his fine yacht.

Liam said little apart from the occasional comment about the wind and some questions about how they would reef the sails should the need arise. However most of his thoughts were about the grim prospects which lay ahead. A life on the run, always looking over his shoulder, wondering when he'd be hauled in front of Pearse, ostensibly to explain his actions but in reality to receive his death sentence. He'd welcomed the opportunity to join Pat and Anne in their flight from Northern Ireland but for him it was out of the frying pan into the fire. At least he was helping them escape to the South and although they would continue to be hunted by Irish Intelligence they had friends who would shelter them and more important, they would no longer have the British Army searching them. If captured by the Irish the worst Pat could expect would be a lengthy jail sentence but if the Brits caught him it would mean the death penalty. He glanced across at his two companions and smiled at them. They had believed him about the truth drug and they were now the only friends he had in the whole world. If he did nothing else, he would do everything he could to help them.

Two hours into their voyage and the wind had headed them to the point where Pat would shortly be forced to decide whether to come about and tack in towards Magilligan Strand or continue on port tack in a northwest direction towards Malin Head. The Inishowen lighthouse now stood well proud of the horizon and its light briefly illuminated their red sails every twenty seconds giving Pat something else to worry about. They weren't carrying any navigation lights so it was unlikely that the lighthouse keeper was aware of their presence but if they were spotted, what then? Seafaring prudence suggested tacking inshore first but that meant passing the lighthouse only a mile or away so he chose to remain on port tack and although that would take them further offshore it reduced the risk of being spotted. A strong westerly wind would start to kick up a sea the further offshore they were driven and it conditions worsened to the point where the could no longer sail to windward then they'd be in danger of being swept out to sea. If that happened the very best they could hope for would be getting rescued by the Portrush lifeboat who wouldn't look kindly on them but after that? He shuddered at the consequences of being captured by the Brits. It would be the end of their dreams.

'The wind has headed us a bit but we'll stay on this tack and hopefully in a mile or two we might be out of view from the lighthouse, at least we'll be further away and harder to see. When dawn comes we should be able to see the gaps in the cliffs and if we can't get ashore at the first beach then the back up is the larger beach at Culdaff but that's another five or six miles up the coast towards Malin Head.' Said Pat by way of information. He was not inviting a debate on his plan.

'What if we can't land at Culdaff?' Asked Liam.

'I'm afraid after that there are only cliffs all the way to Malin Head - not somewhere I want to be in a westerly.' He replied starkly.

The wind continued to increase and from time to time Pat was forced to feather the main during the stronger gusts. They were sitting as far out on the windward side-deck as they could but the boat still heeled until her gunwale was under water and half way up the leeward side-deck. He knew they ought to take in a reef but that would be a lengthy process during which they'd drift a long way downwind making it even more of a struggle to get to the beach. It was an agonising decision because they were now only a couple of miles from the bay which was clearly visible in the pre-dawn light. So he fought on but the closer they got the cliffs the fiercer the gusts and between them there were times when the wind almost stopped. In the gusts the yacht lay on her side until the water was coming into the boat over the cockpit coaming and Pat was forced to round up into the wind. Then as the gust ended the boat would swing violently upright and over to windward forcing the three of them to dive back into the boat from the sitting-out position. They'd no sooner be crouching down inside the cockpit again when the next gust would come barrelling down from the cliffs and they'd be hanging out as far as they could again. It was now do-or-die. To take in a reef in the mainsail in those conditions would take at least fifteen minutes and possibly much longer during which time they would drift a further mile offshore, so he hung grimly and painfully slowly they clawed their way to windward.

'We'll have to sail past the beach and then come about and approach it on starboard tack.' Yelled Pat, 'this will be our first and hopefully our last tack so let's make sure we get it right. I'll bring her head to wind and then ease her out onto the other tack. Liam, you handle the jib and I'll look after the main. Anne, you keep your head down and when the boom flies across to the other side you must sit out on the side deck as quickly as possible. Fortunately there are no waves to speak of so I'll drive her straight up onto the beach and as soon as she hits the bottom we jump out and run for the dunes. OK?'

'OK.' Replied Anne and Liam in unison as they braced themselves for the final act in the drama.

Glancing repeatedly over his left shoulder as they sailed past the beach he waited until he was sure they could lay the middle of the strand and then he shouted loudly, 'Right then - lee ho!' He pushed the tiller away from him to bring the boat up to windward but as they came through the eye of the wind the heavy boom swept violently across the deck catching Anne on the head with a sickening thud and knocking her unconscious. The sails filled on the opposite tack when another gust blasted down from the cliffs and as it pressed the boat hard over on its side Pat watched in terror-struck slow-motion as his unconscious lover tumbled headlong into the sea. Helplessly he cried out in anguish, 'Anne's gone overboard!' But Liam had seen everything. In an instant he let the jib fly and dived headfirst into the sea. With the sails flapping violently Pat flung the yacht back into the wind as Liam swam as fast as he could back to Anne who was afloat but lying forward with with her face in the water. When he reached her Liam grabbed her hair and pulled her head backwards out of the water but without a life jacket he was struggling in his sodden clothes to keep his own head above water. Meanwhile Pat bore away on starboard tack and freeing the sheets completely the boat lay broadside to the wind with violently flapping sails and they slowly drifted leewards down toward Liam and Anne. The few seconds it took to get to them felt like an eternity for Pat. 'Why now?' He thought. They were no more than a half mile from safety when this disaster had struck but as the boat drifted towards them he realised he might just have a second chance. Leaning out over the stern as they drifted past, he grabbed Anne's life jacket by the shoulder straps and with the strength of desperation he hauled her onto the after-deck where she lay like a stranded fish gasping for breath. 'Hang on Anne!' he yelled as she began to regain consciousness, 'I need to help Liam.' But when he turned to where he'd last seen Liam he had vanished. 'Liam!' he screamed with all his might, 'Liam!' But there was no reply, only the violently flogging sails and the sound of the wind moaning in the rigging. Liam was gone. It was the ultimate sacrifice, he had drowned in the act of saving Anne's life. Pat knew that without any buoyancy aid and fully clothed Liam would have had great difficulty simply keeping himself afloat. Somehow he must have overcome the animal instinct to hang onto her in the hope that her jacket could support them both. His death was not an accident, Liam must have known he was risking his life the instant he made the decision to dive overboard after Anne.

These thoughts were swilling around inside his head as he gathered in the mainsheet. *'I'm going to have to gybe around and then sail her in on the mainsail Anne. You must crouch down as low as you can because the boom is going to whip across violently and...'* he was in mid-sentence when a grim-faced Anne interrupted him, *'Get on with it Pat, I'm not going to make that mistake again!'*

The boat crashed through the gybe and a measure of calm returned. As he hardened in on the mainsheet and brought her back onto the wind the boat leant over and gathered way. Anne grabbed the jib sheet and started to haul it in when Pat shouted, *'Don't worry about that now - we're going to make it to the beach on the mainsail. Just hang on and get ready to jump ashore.'*

The weather gods relented and the wind eased as they entered the centre of the bay. Gratefully Pat scanned the water ahead and seeing no rocks he yelled, *'Anne, this is it. When we hit the sand I'm hoping she won't come to a sudden stop but please hang on tightly just in case.'* The words had barely left his lips when they both noticed a slight slowing and then gradually and almost gracefully the yacht slid to a halt. Pat immediately leapt overboard into water that barely reached his waist and grabbed Anne as she clambered over the side-deck and then, with strength unknown he carried her in his arms to the edge of sand and gently set her down. They embraced tightly and he cupped her face between his hands kissed her. Then they ran hand-in-hand to the back of the beach and the shelter of the sand-dunes where they flopped down in the stillness and looked back. The rising sun was bathing the high cirrus clouds in swathes of pink, red and purple and its spilled gold pathway glimmered and glittered on the sparkling sea. Silhouetted blackly against the brightness the yacht that had brought them to safety looked sad and abandoned as it leant over in a gust of wind which rolled down from the hills behind them and passed undetected overhead. Trying to free itself from the sand the sad yacht turned and twisted restlessly under the flogging sails while they watched from their quiet place under the dunes.

'I can't leave her like that Anne.' Said Pat as he hauled himself to his feet. 'You stay here.' Standing in the water beside the boat he took off his life jacket and pushed it safely under the foredeck. He lowered the gaff, secured it to the boom. He and tightened up the mainsheet to keep the boom from swinging, Next he lowered the jib which he un-hanked and stuffed beneath the foredeck. Now there were no clues as to the drama that had been played out within a half mile of the beach. Completely undamaged, she'd be ready to go to sea again when the tide came in and she floated off. Satisfied with his work he stroked her bows, noticing her name for the first time - 'Niamh' was engraved in a traditional Irish font on a small wooden plaque beneath the bows on both port and starboard sides and the letters had been lovingly painted white by a proud owner. From somewhere deep in his memories he had a flash-back from his school days. He was sitting in the classroom, wide-eyed as the teacher told them a story from the depths of Irish mythology, 'Niamh means radiance, lustre or brightness. She was the daughter of Manannan, the god of the sea and she was known as 'Niamh of the Golden Hair'. She was the lover of poet-hero Oisin and together they lived in Tir-na-nOg, the land of eternal youth.' Tears welled up in his eyes, 'What a beautiful name,' he said to himself, 'if we ever have a daughter, that's what we'll call her and every time we say her name we'll remember what we owe to this boat.'

He returned to find Anne sound asleep on the sand. His heart overflowed with love for this wonderful girl who lay there soaked to the skin, still wearing her life jacket but sleeping like a baby. For the first time in his life he felt responsible for someone other than himself. This was truly the first day of the rest of his life and he knew that from now onwards he would devote himself totally to keeping Anne safe, healthy and happy.

As he watched an involuntary shiver stirred her and she slowly opened her eyes and smiled at Pat who was standing above her. 'Crickey Pat, we're alive - we made it...' but before she could finish her sentence she was overtaken by uncontrollable sobbing. He knelt down beside her and lifted her until her head rested in his lap. There was nothing he could say so he waited until her body was still again and then, choosing his words carefully said, 'Anne, Liam gave his life to save us both and now we owe it to him not just to survive but to be happy, bring up a family and make sure that we never, never forget the sacrifice he made. Whatever guilt he may have felt from his drug-induced betrayal has been atoned and moreso. If any man deserves to be in heaven, it's him.' By the time he'd finished the sentence he knew what they would call their son, should they be fortunate enough to have one.

'Now we're going to have to chance our luck with one of those farms on the hill. It wouldn't surprise me if our adventure hasn't already attracted attention.' He said as he hauled them to their feet. Unbuckling her life jacket and lifting it over her head gave him the opportunity to kiss her, afterward he licked his lips and laughed, 'Is that salty lipstick you're wearing?' She grinned broadly and replied, 'We look a right mess don't we? I hope the locals will take pity on us.'

He dropped Anne's lifejacket off at the boat and suddenly feeling very tired the pair climbed back over the the dunes and found their way through a patch of dense, scrubby vegetation which snatched angrily at their sodden clothing. It was with some relief when they finally emerged into a grassy field where a flock of sheep were grazing peacefully. Unused to visitors all their heads lifted to watch as they walked across the short distance to a gate in the hedge which bordered a rough track cutting across the fields beneath the farm. By the time they had reached the bottom of the track leading up to the farmhouse, a man and a woman were waiting at the top to greet them. Pat glanced back and yes, as he expected, the farmer and his wife must have seen everything. Realising he had no idea how to explain their arrival he was left with no other option than to see how the conversation developed and play it by ear.

'You poor things,' said the farmer's wife warmly and with obvious concern, 'come away in and we'll get you some sweet tea while you sit in front of the fire - you must be frozen.' She ushered them into their dark kitchen where the welcome warmth of the black stove against one wall hit them as they entered. A large kettle was already boiling and within minutes they were huddled in front of the stove with blankets over their shoulders drinking steaming mugs of strong, sweet tea.

'Welcome to our home,' said the farmer, 'please tell us what we can do to help you? Your boat will be high and dry soon but when the tide returns we'll need to secure her - either haul her up the beach above the high-water mark or.......will you be moving on somewhere?'

Touched by his sincerity and kindness, Pat introduced himself and Anne and while doing so had no difficulty in deciding to be honest about their predicament. He didn't have to tell the whole story but somehow in the face of such genuine hospitality it was inconceivable to lie. 'We're not planning to do any more sailing just now,' he replied, 'I'll need to make a telephone call at some point so I'm hoping there's a kiosk somewhere nearby?'

'The nearest one is in Culdaff but that's not far and I can take you there on the tractor later - but what about your boat?' He questioned, 'If we're going to make her safe I'll need to get a couple of the local boys to help us pull her up the beach. I'm sure most of the farmers will have seen your drama. We're all early risers here you know.'

Pat looked across at Anne whose eyelids were drooping as she gradually succumbed to the warmth, the safety and the tea. Seeing how he looked at her the farmer's wife said, *'I'm going to take Anne upstairs and get her into bed while you men do what you need to do.'*

Overwhelmed by their generosity and concern he felt tears welling up in his eyes, *'How can we thank you enough for being so kind?'*

'Away with you Pat, I'm sure you'd do the same for us.' She said as she gently helped Anne out of her seat and steered her towards the narrow wooden staircase.

Wiping his eyes he turned to the farmer, *'I don't know what to say, what did we do to deserve such hospitality?'*

The farmer shook his head dismissively and said, *'You've obviously been through hell m'boy tell me all about it as we go down to the boat. At the very least we can bring a warp from her up to the rocks and if you're planning to stay here we can head over to that farm there...'* and he pointed across towards a small cluster of buildings about a half mile away, *'...they've got two strappin' sons who could probably carry the boat up the beach above the high-water mark on their own.'*

Several hours later they returned to the farm where bread and cheese had been set out on the table for lunch. There was no sign of either Anne or the farmer's wife. Pat had done as the farmer had suggested and with remarkable ease the four of them had dragged the boat well above the line of dried-out wrack and various other bits of detritus which defined the high-water mark. In the meantime he'd explained that he was being pursued by the B-Specials as a suspected IRA sympathiser and rather than face internment he and Anne had stolen the boat in Portrush and sailed to Donegal to evade prison. What he'd told them was true but it wasn't the whole truth, however his story immediately engendered support and confirmed that he was among friends who would not inform the Irish Intelligence. Unsurprisingly they'd all heard of the fruitless raid on the Greencastle trawlers but when asked if he'd anything to do with that, he said no.

'If you know anyone in Portrush, you could maybe tell them that the missing yacht is safe and sound here. They might be able to come and collect her?' said Pat.

'The fishermen in Greencastle will know the Portrush lads for sure. I'll tell them when we're next over the hill.' Replied the farmer.

As he finished the ladies appeared, Anne dressed in the farmer's wife's Sunday clothes and looking alive again. *'Go on, you can hug her if you want, we'll not be embarrassed!'* Said he farmer's wife with a chuckle, then spotting his hesitation she continued, *'...but maybe you'd rather have some lunch first?'*

That afternoon the farmer took Pat to Culdaff where he placed a call to his IRA colleague in Buncrana, *'Sean, I need a favour. Can you come across to Culdaff and collect me and my girl? It's a long story and I can fill you in on the way back.'*

'No problem Pat but it can't be today. I'll borrow a car and see you tomorrow probably about lunchtime. Where are you staying?' Enquired Sean.

'We'll meet you outside the village pub in Culdaff at noon - OK?' He replied, realising he didn't know where they would spend the night. On the way back to the farm Pat explained the arrangement and asked about accommodation in the village.

'And why would you be wanting accommodation in Culdaff? Sure you're welcome to stay with us. Our children emigrated to America in '38 so there's a spare bedroom. It would be grand to have the company, you see we don't get many visitors these days.' Said the farmer, *'and if your pal is collecting you from Culdaff, don't worry I'll take you over, although you'll have to sit in the trailer.'*

'We could walk...'

'Nonsense. Me and the missus can do some shopping in Culdaff at the same time.' Said the farmer as they chugged back to the farm with Pat perched on the back of the tractor.

The following morning after breakfast and before the scheduled rendezvous in Culdaff, Pat and Anne walked hand-in-hand down to the beach for one last goodbye to the boat that had carried them safely to freedom. It was a calm morning with a clear blue sky and the sun already high above the horizon to the south east. Flies buzzed and birds sang in the hedges as the made their way to the beach where Niamh was lying on her side on the soft sand above the high tide mark. It was a sombre moment as they looked out to sea and thought about Liam and how he'd made the ultimate sacrifice. Almost without thinking they started gathering stones and piling them into a small cairn near the boat.

'We'll probably never return here Anne,' said Pat softly, *'but we will never forget this place nor will we ever forget what Liam did.'* There was a long pause before he continued, *'so we owe it to him to be happy, don't you think that's what he wanted?'*

'Yes Pat, I agree - but where can we be happy? where can we find peace?' She replied wistfully.

The following day they said goodbye to the farmer and his wife, thanking them for their unquestioning hospitality and promising to come back one day. Sean met them outside the pub in Culdaff as arranged and two hours later they were back in Buncrana drinking an early pint of Guinness in Roddins Bar and three days after that it was another pint of Guinness in the Beggars Bush in Dublin. The IRA had continued to pay the rent on his flat so at least they had somewhere to stay but his job at the Irish Steam Packet Company had not been kept for him as promised. Their excuse was that much of the work they did was for the Irish Government and they'd been put under pressure to make sure that no suspected IRA members were employed. No names had been mentioned but the company felt that it would be too risky to re-employ Patrick McGonigle at this time. They did say that as soon as things quietened down they might reconsider giving him his old job back but that was too open-ended for Pat and Anne who were rapidly running out of funds.

While discussing their limited options in the bar one night, who should walk in but Pearse Kelly. He was wearing his priest's habit and dog collar and recognising Pat and Anne immediately he came over to their table, shook Pat's hand vigorously and gave Anne a kiss on the cheek.

'Wonderful to see you both again,' he said with genuine enthusiasm, 'I lost track of your movements after the air raid - in fact for a while I thought you might have been killed. I know you lost your mother Anne and you have my deepest sympathy.'

'Thank you Father. It was an awful raid and if we'd left the pub fifteen minutes earlier we'd also have been killed. We were only a couple of hundred yards away when the bomb landed on our house.' Said Anne.

It was a quiet time in the bar and during the following hour they related their separate stories. Pearse was impressed by their escape in the yacht and his face darkened when he heard that Liam had drowned. 'Probably for the best.' Was his only response. Pearse was sparing in the details of his flight from the North but through his extensive contacts on both sides of the border he had successfully relocated his arsenal of German arms and then crossed into the South at Derry. He'd only arrived in Dublin a few days ahead of Pat and Anne.

'What are your plans?' he asked, 'Both of you did a great job for the cause and we owe you. If there is anything I can do for you please let me know.'

On an impulse Pat looked across at Anne and took her hand, 'Father, would you marry us?'

'Aren't you supposed to ask me first.' Said Anne, pretending to be shocked.

'It would be an honour - and also my first marriage service since I became a priest!' He responded with a chuckle, 'just name the day.'

That evening in Pat's small flat they talked late into the night about how they might find a peaceful place to live and start a family. Anne thought that maybe they could return to Donegal and start their new life as farmers but neither of them had any experience of working the land and although it had seemed idyllic during the brief time they'd been with the farmer and his wife, they knew it wasn't a practical idea. Europe was aflame and Ireland was balancing on the razor's edge of its neutrality. It felt like it was only a matter of time before either the Germans or the British invaded.

'Maybe we could go to America?' Questioned Anne.

'Great idea, but how?' Said Pat and then added, *'maybe I should talk to Pearse and see if he has any ideas.'*

Exactly a month later a young married couple were leaning over the railings of the Portuguese steamship Serpa Pinto as it slowly pulled out of Lisbon on the weeklong voyage to New York. She was an old ship who showed her age but that matter little to the passengers, most of whom were people like the McGonigles who were fleeing from Europe to start a new life in America. As the boat left the docks and headed out in the broad ocean, a long round of applause sounded from the passengers who had assembled along the rails to bid goodbye to the old world.

'We've a lot to thank the IRA for Anne. If they'd not paid for our tickets, we'd have had to sit out the war in Ireland.' Said Pat as the boat gently lifted to a long ocean swell.

'Yes, but I think we earned it, don't you?' She replied, squeezing herself closer as he reached his arm across her shoulder.

For a while they were silent and then Pat said, *'It's rather nice to think that this old lady was built in 1914 by Workman, Clark and Company in Belfast and now she's taking us to our new life in America.'*

EPILOGUE

On a cold and fresh spring morning in 1948 a family of four disembarked from a TWA Constellation at Shannon Airport after the long flight from New York via Gander in Newfoundland. They were tired but by the time they had walked to the terminal across the tarmac the fresh Irish air had revitalised them. Having cleared customs and collected their baggage they made their way to the exit where a chauffeur driven Riley RMB 2.5 Saloon was waiting for them. The porter loaded their luggage into the boot and they set off on the long drive north to Sligo where they stopped overnight. The following day they left after breakfast and continued north through Donegal to Tremone Bay, a tiny farming community above a sandy beach. With the bay to themselves they spread out a tartan rug and unpacked a wicker hamper containing their lunch then, while they ate their sandwiches the father told them the story of their escape to Donegal while the two children listened wide-eyed. *'So that's why I'm called Liam,'* said the son beaming with pride. *'And that's why my name is Niamh,'* said his younger sister, equally proud.

They finished their lunch but before returning to the car they all added stones to the crude cairn that had remained virtually unchanged during the eight years that had passed since it was built. There was no sign of the boat and sadly the farm above the beach was abandoned. That evening they returned to their hotel in Sligo and the following day the couple made arrangements for their children to be looked after at the hotel while they went for the short drive to a small pier on the shore of Lough Gill where a boatman was waiting to take them across to the a tiny wood-clad island. In its centre there was a small clearing in the trees with a simple wooden seat and a plaque commemorating the life of William Butler Yeats. They sat down and as she rested her head on his shoulder he softly recited Yeats' famous poem again.

'I will arise and go now, and go to Innisfree,
And a small cabin build there, of clay and wattles made;
Nine bean-rows will I have there, a hive for the honey-bee,
And live alone in the bee-loud glade.

And I shall have some peace there, for peace comes dropping slow,
Dropping from the veils of the morning to where the cricket sings;
There midnight's all a glimmer, and noon a purple glow,
And evening full of the linnet's wings.

I will arise and go now, for always night and day
I hear lake water lapping with low sounds by the shore;
While I stand on the roadway, or on the pavements grey,
I hear it in the deep heart's core.'

'We have found peace, haven't we?' Said Anne.
'Yes we have my darling.' He replied, squeezing her tightly.

THE END

Printed in Poland
by Amazon Fulfillment
Poland Sp. z o.o., Wrocław

57456407R00080